Pete

Thanks for
your support

Jay Crowley

12-21

1

LAHONTAN CITY

JAY CROWLEY

ALSO BY JAY CROWLEY

Natalie Adventures – Middle Grade

Cabin in the Meadow

A Ship in the Desert

Opal

Laura

My Selections of Short Stories

A Gift from Nate-Story of a Double Lung Transplant

Not Worthy-Story of Revenge

Maggie

Drum of Hope

ANTHOLOGIES

Other Realms I & II

Heard it on the Radio

13 Bites III & IV

Free for All

From Outer Space MK II & III

559 Ways to Die

The Collapse Directive

Tales of Southwest

Relationship Add-Vice

Christmas Lites VII, VIII, and IX

AWARDS

Who's Who of Emerging Authors 2020

National Novel Writing Month for 2017, 2018, and 2019

I, Jay Crowley, Writer...due out in November

This story is a work of fiction. The places may be real, but not the people. All names and events are products of the author's imagination. Any resemblance to actual names or persons (living or dead) or events is purely coincidental and must not be construed as being real. The research for the story came from Wikipedia, Google and Nevada Mines, Diane Barndt, friends, and my memories.

For updates on new stories and more information on the author,

Email: jaycrowleybooks@gmail.com

Facebook: Jay Crowley-Sweet Dreams Books

Web site www.sweetdreamsbooks.com

If you have enjoyed any of my books -- please take the time to go to Amazon or my Facebook page right now and leave a review of the book or books you have read. It would mean so much to me.

Thank you.

Dedication

I dedicate this book to all my readers.

A writer has many people who help in writing a book. I couldn't do it without my beta reader, Josie. My husband, who cooks dinner while I write, Michelle and family who have to listen to me talk about the book.

Also, I want to give credit to Diane Barndt for the information about the ghost town of Hot Creek. Her husband, a third-generation Nevadan, grew up there.

Enjoy.

Chapter One

Tim Ryan lays crunched at the bottom of the hole. He was knocked out by the fall for a minute or so. Shaking his head to get his senses back, he noticed he was bleeding. Tim had fallen in what looked like an abandoned outhouse hole and landed on something sharp. Looking around trying to get his bearings, he noted that there's all kinds of junk down here.

Checking himself out, he had cut his chest on the left side. Tim, thankfully, had worn his lined Carhartt jacket, which now had a rip. *Darn, brand new coat.* However, the cut was bleeding pretty good. Taking a wraparound scarf from his neck, he secured it around his chest to help stop the bleeding. Now to figure how to get out of this hole, as he was a good seven to eight feet down.

Tim called for his four-year-old pit-bull Caesar, who had a brown spot on top of his head, that looked like a crown. Caesar appeared at the top of the hole and looked down at his master, wagging his tail. Tim gave the command, "stay Caesar." Tim didn't want the dog wandering off or chasing rabbits.

Well, this was a heck of a predicament. The ground was hard, so Tim thought maybe he could make steps in the outhouse wall to get out as there were no tree roots. *Dang, he was still bleeding.* It was fairly dark, so he couldn't see what had cut him.

Tim stood there for a moment, contemplating what to do. *Does anybody know he's here?* Tim couldn't remember if he told anybody he was going out prospecting with his metal detector. He looked at his cell phone, no signal, but it did give light in the hole. What cut him was a jagged piece of glass from a large pickle jar with something inside. *Darn, there sure is a lot of stuff down here.*

Since his retirement, fifty–eight year old, Tim didn't plan much out. He did things on the spur of the moment. This Saturday morning on a whim, he and Caesar decided to take their metal detector and go to Lahontan City, located across from the Lahontan Dam, between Chruchhill mile marker 50 and 51 on the way to Fallon, about thirty miles from his home. Tim and Caesar like to go to see what they can find.

However, seeing it's early Spring, it wasn't such a good idea. Plus, there's been heavy rains, *which is probably why the ground gave way.* This also means, sadly, not a lot of people out camping or fishing yet, limiting the ability to find him in this hole.

He thought, *thank goodness there's no snakes down here, I hate snakes. Dang, I can't get the bleeding to stop. It's not bad, but it's annoying.* He started to laugh to himself, *well, I guess I'm in a pickle...*

Tim took his knife and started carving toe holes in the wall. Caesar began a growling type of bark, "Is there somebody out there, boy?" asked Tim. Caesar stayed by the hole and started to growl. Then he started a more vicious growl.

"Hello, is someone down there?" came a woman's voice from a distance.

Tim yelled back, "yes, I fell in this hole, and I'm bleeding. Do you have a rope?"

The voice came back, "yes, in my truck, I'll be right back."

It seemed like forever before she came back. Tim heard a vehicle drive up, and Caesar started growling again. Tim said, "it's OK, boy, they're here to help me."

Ceasar gave a snarl. "Your dog won't let me near the hole," said the voice.

"Ceasar, it is OK," yelled Tim.

The dog backed away from the hole. And the woman dropped the rope. "Can you tie it to something?" asked Tim.

"Yes, I drove my truck over. "I'll tie it to the winch and pull you out." Tim grabbed the broken pickle jar. To his surprise, it was heavy. He was curious about what was inside, but for now, he placed it in his jacket, tying it to his waist. Tim also slipped his belt through the handle of the metal detector. Wrapping the rope around him, he yelled, "I'm ready."

11

He heard her start the truck, and the winch began pulling him up. He was about halfway up when something caught his attention off to the left. He glances over to see a human head, *and by damn, it looked like it turned to look at him.* "Holy crap," Tim said out loud as he hurriedly climbed out of the hole.

Caesar was all over Tim, as Tim loved him up. "Well, that's something I don't want to go through again. Thank you so much. Not sure how I can thank you. Also, not to alarm you, I need to call the authorities, as there's a human head down in the hole."

The woman said, "Wow, a human head?" as she shivers, "I'm glad I was here to help. What is that you brought up in your jacket?"

Tim says, "I don't know, it looked like a pickle jar, and it's old. Apparently, someone threw it down the outhouse many years ago. I need to call the authorities. Seeing as I have no cell service, I'll use the radio in my truck."

Walking off to his truck, he also wanted to put his stuff away. While placing the jar in the truck, Tim looked it over. *It's heavy. There is a piece of cloth inside, and whatever it is, it's sure is dirty. I'll clean it up when I get home.* Tim covered the jar with a blanket on the back seat floor of the truck and proceeded to radio the authorities.

Tim walked back, "The sheriff should be here in a bit, no hurry as it's a skeleton head, it's looking like it has been there a while."

The woman stated, "you're bleeding. Let me bandage you up," she says, going to her truck for the first aid kit.

"Wow, you're like Superwoman and Florence Nightingale. I am so glad that you showed up. By the way, my name is Tim Ryan, what is yours? Seeing you're bailing me out here."

The woman laughs, "Hi, I'm Sherri." She hesitated and never gave her last name.

"What brought you out here in April?" Asked Tim.

"I love to come here, and I usually bring my metal detector and probe to find outhouses, looking for old bottles," confessed Sherri.

"Well, here is an outhouse hole for you. Instead of burying it, it looks like they covered with timbers, that just happened to give way with me on it." Tims laughs. "You might find bottles down there as there's lots of junk, plus a man's head."

Tim paused for a minute, "Seeing it's a rather deep hole, It might have been a communal outhouse, with lots of people using it. Thank goodness that stuff had deteriorated," they both laughed.

Before Tim walked back to his truck holding his side, he asked, "Would you let me buy you lunch? It's the least I can do. I'll notify the Sheriff where I'll be if they have questions."

Sherri thought about it for a moment, "Yes, that would be great, but Fallon is probably the closest."

"I know a great Mexican restaurant, Las Fiesta, in Fallon," suggested Tim.

"I am quite familiar with it as I live in Fallon. Plus, you might want to stop by ER about that cut. From being in an outhouse, with all the stuff and all, you could get an infection," replied Sherri.

"Good point, but let's go eat first," with that word, Ceasear ears perked up.

Chapter Two

Tim and Sherri talked for two hours or more about everything. The day was incredible. Tim couldn't believe how much they had in common. They both were widowed and recently retired. Sherry was a history teacher and a part-time librarian. Tim, a highway engineer for the Nevada Department of Transportation.

The only difference they had, Sherry was into cats, and course Tim had Caesar, his pit bull. They agreed to meet again in Lahontan City next Saturday, weather permitting, and go metal detecting/bottle digging together.

Hopefully, not falling into any outhouses. Sherry was looking forward to inspecting the hole Tim had fallen into after the authorities were through. Maybe, next week, they would find some great bottles at the bottom. She could only surmise.

Before they left the restaurant, Tim ordered two tacos for Caesar as he knew by now the dog was hungry and needed to go potty. As he walked around the corner across from the restaurant to his parking spot and saw his truck, Tim knew something was wrong. Ceasar was sitting up and barking. He never does that, as he usually sleeps until Tim gets back. Tim had parked in the shade of the Elk Club building and left him water. He always locked his vehicle because of Ceasar.

Sherri had parked in front of the restaurant, so he assumed she was gone already.

Tim opened the door, and Ceasar almost knocked him down to get out. Tim grabbed him, "It's okay, boy. What is the problem?" as he petted Ceasar, he calmed down.

Looking around, he notices a group of kids way down the block. The tonneau cover on the truck had been opened. "What the heck?" He looked inside. The metal detector was still there, but the lid of his ice chest was disturbed. It didn't look like anything was missing. *Must have been those kids looking for beer,* he thought.

Letting Ceasear go potty, Tim came around and looked in the cab on the rear passenger side floor, and the jar was still there under a blanket. Seeing everything was okay, he yelled, "come on, boy, get your treat." Ceasar hopped in the back seat, devouring the tacos.

As Tim got into his truck, he felt his side ache. *I guess I better go to the ER.* He drove over to the small hospital in Fallon, and it wasn't busy. Parking in the shade and locking the truck, he went inside and talked to a receptionist named Bruce, telling him about his accident. After filling out the paperwork, Bruce said, "Have a seat, and the nurse will come and get you."

Tim looked at a magazine from the table, Sports Illustrated Swim edition, *not bad.* Shortly, a nurse came out and called his name. "Tim."

He quickly hustled over to her and noticed her name tag, Tina, as they walked down a hall and into a little room. "How can I help you today?

Tim laughed and said, "Well, Tina, you are not going to believe this, but I fell into an outhouse hole and got cut." Lifting his shirt, the cut was no longer bleeding, just oozing. Sherri had used butterfly bandages. The nurse looked, "This will require stitches. I will get the Doctor."

Tim sat in the little room looking at all the graphic pictures on the wall, some on heart problems, arthritis in the legs, and immunization shots for kids. One sign got him laughing, "You have a 99% chance of getting shingles after 50." *Well, I passed fifty and haven't caught them yet.*

What seemed like an hour was only a few minutes before the Doctor arrived in the examination room.

"Hi Tim, I'm Doctor Barnes. I understand you have a cut and may need some stitches? In cases like this, can you tell me how this happened? It's police protocol."

"Ha-ha, No, I wasn't in a bar fight. I wish I had a great story to tell you, but I fell into an abandoned outhouse hole out at Lahontan City and got cut on a piece of broken glass, probably from an old pickle jar," sighed Tim.

The Doctor smiled, "an old pickle jar, really? Wonder what it was doing in an outhouse and not the dump?" As he cleaned the wound, he injected lidocaine. He explained, "that shot was to deaden the cut for the sutures." As he opens the suture kit, he took a needle out to sew up the wound. "Even though it's a superficial cut, it will need about five stitches to help it heal. My main concern is infection."

Tim grinned and bared the sutures, "I assume someone dumped the jar down the hole maybe by mistake, many years ago, as it looks old. However, there was a lot of junk down there, including a human head."

"Interesting, Wow, a human head. I go out to Lahontan City now and then looking for bottles, so I am glad you found the head and not me," he laughed. "The workers did a lot of drinking back in those times, so there are some great bottles," the Doctor explained. "There you go, good as new. Just keep it clean and covered."

Reaching into a drawer, he handed Tim a tube of medicine. "Keep this salve on the cut for a few days. If any signs of infection appear, get to a doctor."

"Thank you, Dr. will do," replied Tim.

Chapter Three

Tim brought the jar in the house so that he could get a good look at it. Taking it to the kitchen sink, he used Dawn soap to clean it up on the outside as he suspected that it was amalgam in the jar.

Tim grew up around mining and was familiar with amalgam. There also was an old shammy with a map sitting on top of the amalgam. Tim had only broken a piece off the lip of the jar, so mainly the jar was intact, just heavy from the amalgam.

Tim thought, *Wow, amalgam is a mixture of mercury and gold. There's maybe thirty ounces of gold in the jar. In today's markets, thirty times, I think gold is going for around one-thousand-eight-hundred an ounce, which equals about fifty-five thousand dollars... Wow, worth the cut, ha-ha.*

Tim quickly glanced at the map. It was like no map he had seen before. *Wonder where the mine is?* Tim was familiar with the mining industry growing up in a mining family. *Is there a long lost mine out that way? We'll have to check and see. I'll have to go over this map more later. But first, I'm making a copy of the map. This shammy is hard to read. Then I'm putting this jar in the bedroom floor safe with the shammy.*

Tim went into his office, made a copy of the map, and placed it in the office safe. The safe looked like a shelf, even had books on it. No one would ever suspect it was a wall safe.

Tim turned on his computer and figured he would search for information about any mines in the Lahontan area. He also wanted to find out more about Lahontan City and any gold mines associated with the town.

For everything Tim knew from working in that area, the town was built to house the workers and their families. The Feds created Lahontan City, which sprang up almost overnight and disappeared just as fast.

The Federal government wanted to build a dam to reserve water from the Carson River for irrigation. Lahontan City lasted from 1911 to 1915, which was the length of the construction of the Lahontan Dam.

This dam would be important to the Nevada farmers in Fallon, and it was the first federally funded western reclamation project of its kind.

If Tim remembers right, before the building of the Lahontan Dam, the government had tried another construction effort with the Truckee-Carson Project—later to be called the Newlands Project. However, that project became plagued with inefficiency, discontent, drinking, and brawling of the workers.

The Bureau of Reclamation thought if they created a family environment for the workers, it would resolve these problems. Based on this theory, Lahontan City was born.

The City met all the needs of the people. Wooden framed houses or accompanied tents, a medical facility, and even an emergency treatment clinic established with a physician in charge.

A dining hall, I believe, capable of feeding three hundred people per shift, was completed around April 1911. They build a library, plus a small school for the children of the workers. It was a full-service community.

The residents of Lahontan City played as hard as they worked. They spent time fishing and hunting along the Carson River. There was also a bar and a pool hall. However, baseball became the primary sport. The Lahontan boys often played against Fallon and other towns.

The residents with talent formed the Lahontan band. Their music helped with different social functions.

It seems that during its short life, Lahontan City was like any American town. Nonetheless, with the dam completion, all the workers left, leaving it a ghost town and, like so many towns in Nevada, leaving only memories of past glories.

Today only a one stone chimney and a few small stone fireplaces and citrine stand to mark its existence. The desert from which the town sprang has reclaimed Lahontan City. *Of course, there was help from people who tore down the buildings to be used elsewhere,* thought Tim.

Tim thought *it's all fascinating. Nevada has so much history. I must have fallen in the town's communal outhouse.*

Picture of Lahontan City today.

He even found some pictures of what the town looked like in its heyday.

Lahontan City

Another view of the City.

The town even had a train. The famous Carson-Colorado that ran from Carson City to Tonopah and on to California.

Tim thought, *interesting. However, I can't find any information or mention of miners or*

mines. Wonder what area this gold would have come from? Must be Virginia City.

Chapter Four

Tim lives in Moundhouse, about five miles from Carson City, which is the capital of Nevada. He and his wife, Molly, bought the property over thirty years ago and raised three children on the five acres.

Relaxing in his recliner with a beer, Tim reflected on when he met Molly. They met at Marina Cove at Lake Lahontan. Tim was doing engineering work out that way and stopped into the Marina for lunch. There she was, all five feet of her with dark brown hair and gray eyes. Her feisty ways intrigued him. Every day for a week, he went in for lunch before he had the nerve to ask her out. After that, it was fantastic, and she became the love of his life, his soul mate.

Damn, how he misses her. Molly died ten years ago from breast cancer. Their Marina Cove was torn down many years ago to make way for the Lahontan State Park boat ramp on the Lake. So many memories are gone. Tears appeared in his eyes, *enough of this, what's gone is gone, you were lucky to have what you had.*

So now Tim and Caesar take care of the chickens and the place. It has plenty of room for Ceasar to run and keep guard over. The children are all grown, and he is a grandpa three times. They come and visit, but their lives are busy.

Over the years, Tim has become an introvert. He was never interested in dating after Molly's death. Tim felt blessed that he had found his soul mate. He thought you don't have that kind of luck twice. However, today, to his surprise, he had a great time with Sherri.

Tim's property is fenced and gated, mainly to keep wild horses out. Sometimes, Tim opens the gate and lets the horses in. There is a herd of seven horses, and it's a beautiful sight to drink your coffee at the kitchen table and watch the wild animals.

When you live in the country, you also have sensor lights, mainly for the wild animals, like coyotes, bears or deer. A metal gate won't keep bears out. They climb over, and the coyotes and deer jump over. However, the lights make them shy away from the house, so it's a good deterrent.

Tim was still sitting in his favorite chair, watching the evening news before heading to bed. When he noticed the front security lights came on, Ceasear ears perked up, and he growled. Tim hadn't heard a car, and the gates were closed. Tim knew the chickens were locked up and safe. So he got up to look out the kitchen window to see what wild animal was out there.

Tim thought he saw a shadow of a person in the yard. Grabbing his nine-millimeter Glock off the kitchen island, he walked over to the window and watched. Good thing the house was locked up. Tim waited.

The only light on in the house was in the front room by the television. Tim stood in the dark kitchen. Sure enough, it was a man, and he was sneaking up to the house. Ceasar was growling. "It's okay, boy," Tim whispered.

The person tried the front door very gently, found that it was locked. The sensor lights had gone off, which they do if they don't pick up movement.

Tim thought enough of this crap. He yelled through the door, "Get the heck off my property; why you can," he continued to shout, 'I have a gun and a pit bull." Tim heard the guy say something and start running. The sensor light came back on, lighting up the yard. Tim opened the door and went outside with Caesar, who took off running toward the gate. Tim fired a shot in the air just to make sure the person kept running.

What in the heck was that all about? I've never been bothered in thirty years of living here.

The rest of the night, Tim was restless, with one eye open listening for any sound. Caesar was on alert also.

Chapter Five

Tim took the jar of amalgam to an assayer friend of his family in Virginia City to have its analysis.

"Hi Alan, long time no see, " said Tim.

"Hi Tim, yeah, it has been a year or two. What are you up to?"

'Retired now, so taking it easy. However, I came by to have you check out this amalgam I found. Hoping you might be able to tell me a little about it and approximately where it came from." Tim proceeded to tell Alan where he found it.

Alan looked it over and was impressed with the quality and the quantity of the amalgam. He asked Tim, "how much do you have here, and do you want to sell?"

"I think there are about thirty ounces. Don't want to sell right now, maybe later. Want to find out more about it first and where it might have come from," laughs Tim.

Alan took the jar and placed it on the scale. "You were close, as there are thirty-two ounces here. I would say it's old, probably, been in that hole for a hundred years. I'll take a sample and analyze it for you. If you don't mind, I like to put this amalgam in a better container. I don't trust the jar."

"Good point," as they poured the amalgam into an iron flask.

"I would also suggest you take a sample over to the University of Nevada, Mining Department, and have them look at it. They maybe can tell you more about it. If you decide to sell, though, remember I'm interested."

"I'll keep that in mind. Thanks. Alan, would you mind sending the sample to the University to see if they can help us find the location?"

"Sure, will do, play it safe and keep this stuff under lock and key as it's quite valuable."

When Tim got home, that's precisely what he did again. "Wow," said Tim out loud. Placing the iron flask in his safe in the bedroom floor. *Who would have thought? But how did it get in an outhouse in Lahontan City?*

Who would have figured falling into an outhouse hole could lead to some adventure? This is exciting, thought Tim. *Maybe this is why the guy tried to break in? But how would he know I have the gold? Or better yet, where I lived?* Tim thought *for a moment, I had to fill out papers at the Doctors office, giving my address, and they all knew I found a jar. Interesting. I've got to think about all of this. Or maybe I'm making a mountain out of a molehill.*

"Come on, Ceasar, let's get something to eat."

While he and Caesar sat and ate, Tim remembered when he was a kid. *His family had a mine outside of Lousetown, by Virginia City. It was a cinnabar mine. They were all up there one summer day mining when they hit natural, quick, which is mercury in a liquid form. Everyone was*

sealing up the hole and getting iron flasks for the quick. This was liquid gold. In those days, the cinnabar was sent to Winnamuca to be retorted at a high cost. They captured forty flasks of natural quick that day.

Tim smiled to himself. He never got excited about gold, but that day was exciting, and he never forgot the incident.

Chapter Six

Tim hadn't been involved in mining for years, so he thought he would see if they still use mercury to find gold. Turning on his computer, he google amalgam and started reading.

"Mercury is used in gold and silver mining because of the convenience and the ease with which mercury and precious metals amalgamate. In placer mining, the minute specks of gold are washed from sand or gravel deposits. The mercury used to be used to separate the gold from other heavy minerals.

After the practical metal is taken out of the ore, the mercury was sent down a long copper trough, which formed a thin coating of mercury on the exterior. The waste ore is then transferred down the channel, and gold in the waste amalgamated with the mercury. This coating would then be scraped off and refined by evaporation or known as retorting to get rid of the mercury, leaving behind somewhat high-purity gold.

The use of mercury in placer mining is now prohibited, as it has caused extensive pollution problems in riverine and estuarine environments, that is still ongoing to this day."

Yeah, that is why the fish in Carson River have mercury, plus Lake Lahontan, as the Carson River feeds into it.

"Also, amalgam obtained by the heating process in a distillation retort, recovering the mercury for reuse and leaving behind the gold, released mercury vapors to the atmosphere. The process could induce adverse health effects and long term pollution.

Today, mercury amalgamation has been replaced by other methods to recuperate gold and silver from ore in developing nations. Hazards of mercurial toxic waste have played a significant role in the phasing out of the mercury amalgamation processes. However, mercury amalgamation is still regularly used by small-scale gold placer miners (often illegally), particularly in developing countries."

We used to play with the stuff, and I never died. Sometimes, I think it isn't all that bad, but what do I know? Well, enough about the mercury, let's find out about the map. But before that, I'm fixing lunch. "You hungry, boy?"

After lunch, Tim headed back to his office. Tim felt a cold breeze and a real stinky smell. Caesar's ears perked up when they entered the room. They both looked around as they walked in, nothing there. Tim spotted something on his desk blotter. There scribbled in big, bold letters

"BEWARE.'

What is this? Who did this? What in the heck is going on? Beware of what? Tim felt the warm air come back into the room, and the god awful smell left. Both he and Caesar shivered.

Tim shook his head. *Maybe I'm creeped out because of the human skull I found.* The Sheriff's office said it was old. They found that the skull had an indention, so they suspected foul play, but it had been in the hole for at least ninety years or more.

Tim thought back to the day he spotted the skull, *and in his mind, he swears it turned and looked at him. Darn, am I dealing with a ghost now? Now, I wish I never fell in that hole.*

Tim, you have been watching too much TV. It would help if you got out more. Tomorrow, he *was meeting Sherri to go bottle digging. Maybe that would change things.*

As he stood in his office, the phone rang, he nearly jumped six feet. *Calm down, Tim.*

"Hello."

"Hi, Tim, this is Alan. Have some info for you. From what I can gather on the amalgam, it came from somewhere down by Tonopah. Maybe around the Hot Creek area."

"Hot Creek, never heard of it," stated Tim.

"Yeah, it was an old mining town, believe the hotel is still there on a ranch. Google it to get more info. That's all the info I have. I hope it helps. Remember, if you want to sell, let me know."

"Thanks, Alan, for your help. At this point, though, I'm not interested in selling." *Alan knows how much amalgams I have, but I'm not telling anyone else, not yet anyway.*

Tim got off the phone and started googling Hot Creek. *I can't believe I never heard of it.* Sure enough, Tim found a site telling him about Hot Creek, Nevada.

"In early 1867, a small town formed along Hot Creek and was named after the creek, which had been named for the steam that often rose from its surface in the morning. Hot Creek peaked in 1868 when its population was over 300. The town had a hotel, a blacksmith shop, an assay office, and several saloons. The town began to decline in 1868 when new strikes

elsewhere lured most of the 300 residents away. A minor revival took place in 1880 but lasted only one year. New ore discoveries were made in 1897, and some of the people returned. Operations continued until 1912, when mining was abandoned for good. The Hot Creek Ranch Company organized a large ranch encompassing the old Hot Creek townsite. The ranch has been the salvation of the town's remaining buildings. One of the most impressive structures is a stone building that served as a hotel. It was built in 1908. Submitted by: HBC "

Tim thought, Wow, did the gold come from Hot Creek? The timeline fits. Is there still gold in that area that hasn't been found? Is that where this map of the mine comes from? Tim's head was whirling with questions.

Hot Creek Hotel – still stands today

Tim thought *I've got to make a trip down there. I learn something new each day.*

Chapter Seven

Tim was meeting Sherri at ten. He packed lunch with chicken salad sandwiches, chips, and a few beers, plus water. Tim couldn't believe how excited he was to see Sherri again.

They both arrived at the same time. Tim helped her with her gear, and then he got his metal detector. Caesar was excited and running around, looking for rabbits to chase. Caesar saw a couple of big ones, and off he ran. Tim let him run for a bit, then called him in. Rattlesnakes aren't out yet, but you never know.

Tim and Sherri went in separate directions. Tim was cautious that the ground was solid, where he was walking. They were twenty feet or so apart when Tim's detector started beeping.

Sherri came over with her probe and stabbed at the ground. It was soft. Taking her shovel, Tim began to dig. Around two feet, the shovel lightly hit something. Sherri quickly took a hand shovel and carefully dug around the object. "Wow, look at this, it's a lady's leg bottle...awesome. They are worth a few bucks, and it's in great shape. Dirty, but the rice will clean her up," she said beaming.

Tim asked, ' What is a lady's leg bottle?"

"See how the neck of the bottle is shaped like a lady's leg, that is how you tell, " explained Sherri.

"Interesting, and they are hard to find intact?" question Tim.

"Yes, very hard to find. This is a whiskey bottle," stated Sherri.

After a few hours, they didn't find much else of value and sat down on the tailgate of her truck to eat lunch. Sherri had brought salad and cookies. Pouring water into a dish for Ceasar and giving him food for his tummy, he took a nap. Sherri and Tim split a beer and talked about everything. "How is your cut?"

"Doing great, the Dr. did an excellent job. Hurt for a day or two, but now don't even feel it."

"Just for disclosure, Dr. Barnes is my brother-in-law. Fallon is a small town," as she laughed.

"Awesome to have a Doctor in your family. "What other secrets do you have?" laughed Tim.

Sherri blushed and said, "I am a woman of mystery."

Changing the subject. Have you ever heard of Hot Creek, down by Tonopah?" Asked Tim.

"No. What is it?"

"And old ghost town, I would like to go see it? I'm thinking about going down next week. Want to go? We would just go for the day."

Sherri looked at him funny.

"Yeah, I know it is a long trip, but I don't plan on spending, but a couple of hours there. Might be some great bottles. How about going Wednesday?"

She thought for a moment, "It could be fun. Yes, I would love to go."

"Great, we have a date. Pick you up at seven in the morning." and they both smiled. "Of course, I'll need your address."

"How about I meet you at Walmart in Fallon."

"Okay. Walmart it is, seven on Wednesday. Not your home, you are the woman of mystery."

Tim drove home from Lahoton City, humming. *Wow, I have a date, the first one in ten years.*

"What do you think, Caesar?" Who looked at Tim with a pit bull smile.

Chapter Eight

When Tim pulled into the driveway, he knew something was wrong. The picket fence gate was open, which he never leaves open. He wasn't expecting any packages, and those guys know to close the gate. Tim had left the main gate open, but the picket fence gate is always closed to keep the horses out of the main yard.

Caesar jumped out of the truck, his ears perked, and gave a low growl. "Yeah, I know, boy, someone been here. Let's go see what is going on." Tim went to unlock the front door, but it was already unlocked. *What?...* He pulled out his Glock as they stepped inside. The house was in shambles. Cushions off the couch, his chair turned over, papers scattered all over. Tim ran into his office. His computer was still there, things on the floor, the shelve safe was not disturbed, so it looked like nothing was missing.

Caesar ran through the house, but it seems like whoever did this was gone. Tim looked in the bedroom. The safe in the floor wasn't disturbed. They had torn the mattress off the bed, but the gold was safe if that was what they were after.

Tim got on the phone and called the Sheriff's office to report a burglary. *Damn, and I had such a great day and came home to this.*

Two officers came and took pictures and did a report. They dusted for fingerprints but found none. They did find scratch marks on the door, showing where the lock had been picked. "This looks like a professional job. Surprised they didn't take anything," stated officer Brown.

Tim sighed, "Me too, why go to all this trouble looking for something and not take anything? I have nothing of value except my fifty-inch TV and computer. My deceased wife's jewelry I gave to the kids years ago." Tim scratched his head at a loss for what happened. Even though Tim had a pretty good hunch, someone was after the gold or the map.

Finally, the officers left. Tim walked out and shut the front gate. He made sure the picket fence gate was locked. Tim and Caesar shuffled over to close up the chickens for the night... what a day. Now to go pick up the house.

Down the road, a parked car sat in the dark. A lone person was watching Tim's house and listening to a bug that was planted in Tim's office. The listener made it look like a robbery, but the goal was to plant the listening device. The map to the mine was nowhere to be found, so the bug should work. I've got to locate that map.

Tim was cussing as he picked up the mess. What a chore. He got the kitchen and front room back to normal and went to straighten out the bedroom. As Tim walked by the office door, he felt the cold air and that terrible smell, walking inside... *what a mess*. He noticed new scribbling on the desk pad... "**BEWARE,** NOT SAFE IN HERE."

What the hell, what does that mean? The cold air and the smell were still in the office. Caesar gave a low growl. "It's okay, boy. I'm not sure what is going on."

A black felt marker started writing again on the desk pad... "*look in the ivy plant.*"

Tim jumped about six feet when he saw the marker moving on its own. *What in the heck is going on?* But he did as the writing said. Tim walked over to the plant and looked inside. There was a little transistor like a hearing aid. *What the heck??? Someone had bugged my house.* The air in the room got warm again, and he didn't smell the smell. Caesar stopped growling.

Tim said nothing as they quietly walked out of the office and shut the door. *I have to think about this... what is going on? My life is being turned upside down, but by whom? And why? Who knows about the gold? I haven't told a soul. Well, except Alan, and I trust him.*

Chapter Nine

Tim sat at the kitchen table, drinking a cold beer. *What the heck is happening? I'll change the lock tomorrow with a keyless door opener. I need to purchase an inside and outside security system. Who are these people? Worst yet, who is doing the writing? A ghost?* Tim's head was spinning with questions.

"Com'on Caesar, let's go straighten out the bed and crawl into it." Walking back to the bedroom. "I want to sleep on all of this."

Sleep didn't come easy, as Tim's mind wouldn't shut off. Caesar also was restless.

The person in the car saw the lights go off in the house, figuring Tim went to bed. Closing up the listening gear, *there's always tomorrow* as the vehicle drove off.

The next morning, the first thing Tim did was call the locksmith. He would be there around eleven. *That gives me time to go to Home Depot for a security system.* Tim locked up the house, making sure all the windows were locked and put a chain on the front gate with a lock.

Tim never went into the office, just kept the door shut. *I will address that when I come home. I have a plan.*

By midday, everything was accomplished, a new lock on the front door and the security system in place. Tim placed a video in the front room, kitchen, bedroom, and office. Plus, he had a video of the driveway to the garage and the front porch. Best of all, besides taping it, he could watch whatever happens on his cell phone.

Tim started cleaning his office, and as he sat at his desk, he said out loud, "Well, Caesar. I am sorry I landed on that pickle jar and broke it. It could have been worth some money." Tim scratches Caesar's ears. "Maybe we will get lucky when we go to the ghost town this weekend with the map I found. I love to find gold. I have to remember to call the neighbor to feed the chickens." Caesar smiled.

The lone person in the car parked in the shadows, listen to Tim straighten out his office and talk about a trip he was taking this weekend. *Interestingly, he has a map, is it the map to the mine? Sounds like it. I guess I might make a road trip.*

Tim hoped whoever was listening would try to break into the house while he was gone, and he would have him on video.

Chapter Ten

Wednesday morning, Tim was up at five, packed some sandwiches, chips, and cold drinks. He couldn't believe again how excited he was to see Sherri. Caesar, though tired from getting up so early, was all excited as he knew they were going somewhere.

At precisely seven, Tim met Sherri at Walmart. Tim admired how fresh she looked for that time of the morning.

"Hi, how you are doing?" *what a dumb thing to say.*

"Super, though I am not used to getting up this early." They both laughed. "I brought a thermos of coffee and some cups."

"That's great. I brought sandwiches, but never thought of coffee," sighed Tim.

Sherri poured the coffee, placing them in the drink holders as they hopped in their seats.

"This should be an interesting day," stated Tim.

"Yes, I have been looking forward to today."

What did she mean, was she happy to see me or to go on a trip? Tim, you are overthinking. Enjoy the day.

The trip went fast. They talked about her job as a teacher and librarian and his career as an engineer. Their only stop was El Capitan in Hawthorne for them to use the bathroom. Overall, they made good time and were in Tonopah close to eleven. Turning on Highway 6, they headed for Hot Creek. It was around seventy-six miles from Tonopah.

Outside of Warm Springs, Tim pulled over to eat lunch. He parked under a big old cottonwood tree for shade.

"I am not sure how much further it is down the road. Lets stretched our legs and grab something to eat," suggested Tim.

"Sounds great," Sherri said as she hopped out of the truck along with Caesar. Caesar ran around, smelling and peeing on everything.

Looking at the map, "I think we have about thirty-plus miles to go," explained Tim.

Tim thought, *how easy she was to talk to, and how they never seemed to run out of things to talk about and discuss. He could tell she liked him... Boy, this could be interesting.*

They all hopped back in the truck, with their tummy's full. The ride was on a lonely stretch of the road, as they never saw another car. "Wow, doesn't anyone live out this way?" laughed Sherri.

Within the hour, they came to the Hot Creek Ranch off Hot Creek Road.

There was still some old building standing. Tim's cell phone didn't take great pictures. There wasn't much left of the town except the beautiful ranch house that was once the hotel.

On walking into the old hotel −ranch home now, Sherri and Tim signed in the visitor's book. Tim notices she didn't put her last name and address just Fallon, Nevada. Tim spotted a library room with an older man sitting at the desk.

"Hi. Do you live here?" asked Tim.

'Ha-ha, some might think so, as I'm always in here reading everything," stated the man. "My name is Gene, and I give tours of the hotel and the town. What can I do for you?."

"Glad to meet you, Gene, I'm Tim, and this is Sherri. We came to learn the history of this little ghost town."

"Well, you came to the right place, I know just about everything," replied Gene. He started to tell them the history in a monotone.

"Hot Creek is unusual among the mining ghost towns of Nevada. It is at 5546 feet and received all the seasons. It became a settlement around the 1866s. The town was both a mining camp and an essential stop for freight stage traffic to other nearby mining centers like Tybo. The

59

unusual part about Hot Creek was it was also a resort town deep within one of Nevada's most isolated regions." Gene came up for air before he started his story again.

"As the name implies, Hot Creek was built near hot springs, and in the 1800s, these springs were a popular retreat for residents of nearby mining camps. This ornate hotel was built to serve tourists visiting the area. Not much else is known about the settlement, but an 1869 newspaper article mentions an increased interest in the mines in the area."

"Did the Carson-Colorado run nearby?" asked Tim.

"No. That ran from Tonopah, and at that time, about a three-day horse ride from here, " explained Gene.

Sherri had walked off to look over the hotel as the men were talking.

"Gene, did any of the mines around here use amalgam?"

"Funny, why do you ask?" Questioned Gene.

"Well, I found some amalgam that the assayer said may have come from this area," Tim whispered.

"Interesting. There is a story, or maybe a myth that an educated gentleman named Sean Gilroy found a rich gold vein while hard rock mining in these hills using amalgam. No one, as of today, has found the mine.

As the story goes, he was chased out of town for being a womanizer. He didn't care who he wined and bedded, or if they were married or single. Supposedly he had a map of his mine with him and some amalgam when he left town. But it is only a story."

"Did he ever come back to Hot Creek?"

"No, as the story goes, he was last seen down by Lahontan City. But as I said, this is just a story."

"How far is it to Tybo?" asked Tim.

"Only about six miles, not much there anymore, few people still live there." They have tried mining, but too expensive," replied Gene. "While you are here, you should visit it."

61

"Just might do that," stated Tim.

Sherri walked back into the room. Thank you, Gene, for the information, you have been a great help," said Tim as he shook the old man's hand.

"My pleasure, I love to talk about this old town," Gene said with a big smile. "You want a tour of the hotel?"

"Thanks, but not right now, I think we will just look over the outside remains."

They waved goodbye to the gentleman and headed for the truck.

"What an interesting place," sighed Sherri. "The hotel or ranch has beautiful furniture, and everything was so ornate. I saw beautiful pictures of the old hotel and some old bottles," she laughed.

"Agreed, it was quite interesting. I learned a lot today about Hot Creek from Gene. There is a story that a womanizing gent who left Hot Creek and was last sighted in Lahonton City. He was named Sean Gilroy. That may be the body I found... that would be quite interesting, if true."

Sherri turned a little white, "That would be quite interesting if it's true."

"I'll have to research more to find out the facts," stated Tim, a little excited.

Sherri didn't say anything more, just looked out the truck passenger window.

"Do you mind if we go a little further and visit Tybo, it is another ghost town about six miles down the road?" Asked Tim.

"We are here, so let's go."

They saw a State highway sign, and it told them about the town. It was hard to read as it was faded with time., but below is what it said.

TYBO

SILVER - LEAD - ZINC CAMP

EIGHT MILES NORTHWEST OF THIS POINT LIES WHAT WAS FORMERLY ONE OF THE LEADING LEAD PRODUCING DISTRICTS IN THE NATION. PRODUCING ERRATICALLY FROM ORE DISCOVERY IN 1866 TO THE PRESENT (THE LAST MILL CLOSED IN 1937), TYBO HAS MANAGED TO ACHIEVE AN OVERALL CREDITABLE RECORD.

TYBO, IN ITS INFANCY, WAS KNOWN AS A PEACEFUL CAMP, BUT LATER REFUTED THAT CLAIM WHEN THERE OCCURRED RACIAL STRIFE BETWEEN THE IRISH, CORNISH AND CENTRAL EUROPEANS. LATER THESE GROUPS BANDED TOGETHER TO DRIVE FROM THE TOWN A COMPANY OF CHINESE WOODCUTTERS.

THE TOWN WAS NOT UNIQUE IN HAVING THREE RESIDENTIAL SECTIONS, EACH WITH ITS ETHNIC GROUP. HOWEVER, ALL CHILDREN WENT TO THE SAME BRICK SCHOOL.

"Wow, they even had culture wars back then, interesting, " said Tim.

Driving into Tybo was like stepping back in the past. Some of the buildings were being restored, and it looked like a few people did indeed live there.

They got out to walk around, and Caesar went off to pee on everything.

"Wow, look at this building," declared Sherri, taking a picture.

Although they saw no one during the time they were there. One or two of the houses looked lived in, possibly by caretakers of the abandoned property.

Tim said, "Glad we took the time to visit."

"Thank you, I am glad we did too," replied Sherri. "I love these old towns, as they have so much history."

Tim wondered, *is the map of this area? I need to find out.*

Chapter Eleven

They were both quiet on the ride back to Fallon, as it had been quite a day.

"If you are hungry, I will buy dinner?" asked Tim

"Yes. That's sounds good. What did you have in mind?"

"How about a dinner at the Julio's Mexican & Italian Restaurant?" Tim stated. Caesar's ears perked up at the sound of food. Tim looked at his dog and said, "I know, boy, it has been a long day for you and passed your dinner time." Caesar just smiled.

Around six, they pulled into the parking lot. Tim let Caesar out to go pee, and they stretched their legs. "Sorry, the trip was so long, but I learned a lot about Hot Creek, " said Tim, apologizing.

"It was a great day. I got to see the country I had never seen before and with great company."

"Well, thank you, mam, for those kind words." They both laughed. Tim gave Caesar a treat, place water for him as he locked him back in the truck. They walked into the café to fill their tummies.

Chapter Twelve

Tim thought about what he had learned at Hot Creek. Running into that historian was helpful. Now he some idea where the amalgam might have come from and with whom.

Was it possible that his ghost is Sean Gilroy? Shoot, you may not have a spirit, maybe just an active imagination. But what about the writings? Too much to think about for now.

When they drove into the yard, all looked Okay. Caesar ran around and checked everything. Tim locked up the chickens, and then they went into the house. Nothing was disturbed. Tim was glad, as he was tired. *Better, they think I am going away this weekend. Love it when a plan comes together. I will catch you.*

Tim walked into his office, no notes, checking to see if the listening device was still there... it was. *Good. Checking the videos, nothing showed up. All is well.*

Walking into the kitchen, he fixed himself a cup of coffee. Sitting at the table, Tim thought of Sherri. They had set up to meet again on Friday night. *Today was a fun day with her. Maybe I should take this slow. I'm out of my comfort zone, not dating for so long. She seemed to have a good time with him. Shoot, how could she not? He was a good guy, handsome by some definition with his graying temples and blue eyes... ha-ha.*

"Come-on, Caesar, let's watch TV before we go to bed." And two went into the front room.

Around three in the morning, Caesar started to growl, waking Tim up. *What now?* Grabbing his gun, he walked into the kitchen. The security lights were on, and in his front yard was a herd of horses. He had forgotten to shut the gate last night. He laughed to himself, *a little jumpy, aren't we...*

Thursday morning, Tim went out and shut the gate. He had several piles of good horse manure, which he shoveled over by the garden. Caesar ran around checking on everything, as Tim let the chickens out and gathered the eggs.

"Bacon and eggs, for breakfast, boy. Let's go eat."

The kitchen smelled with the aroma of fried bacon and fresh coffee. Tim was content as he ate breakfast. Caesar was also enjoying his scrambled eggs and bacon. Neither had a worry in the world. Life was good.

Now that I have seen Hot Creek, I want to get a good look at that map finally.

Then the phone rang.

Tim wasn't sure to answer, seeing his house was bugged.

"Hello."

"Hey, Dad, this is Mark, was just checking on you."

"Hey, Hey Son, all is well. How about you guys? How is my grandson?"

"We are all fine, just was thinking of you and decided to call."

"I'm so glad you did. Caesar and I have been busy going out to Lahontan City, looking for bottles or whatever treasure I can find. I did meet a nice lady. I know surprise, surprise."

"Wow, that's great, Dad, you need to meet more people. Mom has been gone for a long time. She wouldn't want you to be alone forever."

"Whoa, don't make too much of this. We're just friends," Tim laughed.

"Glad to know all is well. We'll try to visit after school gets out."

"That would be awesome. I need to spoil David before he becomes a teenager."

"Yeah, he'll be thirteen at the end of this year. The time has flown. Well, you take care, and we send our love."

"Love you too, Mark, and say hi to Susan, that great wife of yours," concluded Tim.

Tim hung up the phone, but sat there for a few minutes. He did miss his family. *Now to finally get to look at this map.*

Wow, this looks like a pirate's map. There isn't an ocean around here. Wait, there is a sea serpent in Walker Lake, or so the myth goes, maybe that's it. The boat could also be on Walker Lake or Lake Tahoe so that it could be the serpent, Tahoe Tessie? Or it could just be doodling, to throw you off. The middle of the map looks like the real thing. Wonder where this would be around Hot Creek? Shoot, I have more questions than answers.

Chapter Thirteen

Friday came quickly. Nothing exciting had happened at the house. Tim got dressed to go on his date, as Caesar sat and watched with a pit bull smile. Sherri was coming to meet him in Carson. They were going to Tito's, a Mexican restaurant, for dinner. Tim offered to pick her up, but she said she had business in Carson and would meet him there.

He hadn't quite figured out why she didn't want him to know where she lived or much about her. They were meeting at five. By the time they met, his stomach was growling like Caesar's, as he hadn't eaten all day. *Am I hungry or nervous, one or the other, maybe both?*

Tim wanted to tell Sherri about the map and the amalgam but was hesitant. He didn't know why, but he didn't trust anyone right now.

The conversation over dinner was safe, and Sheri told him she had come to Carson to sell the lady's leg bottle they found for a hundred and twenty-five dollars, so dinner was on her. They had a little disagreement, as Tim reminded her he had invited her to dinner. Sherri relinquished and said dinner was on her the next time. Tim, though, *so we'll have a next time...*

The evening went by fast. Finally, Sherri said, "I have to head home. Thank you so much for the wonderful evening. When are we going bottle digging again?"

"How about Monday?"

Ever so slightly, he noticed a little frown, "You can't do it Sunday?"

"Sorry, but I have plans, as I'm going out of town," explained Tim.

"Okay, then Monday it is. See you in Lahontan City around ten, and I am buying lunch."

"It's a date." They both laughed.

Tim walked Sherri to her truck and hugged her before she drove off. *I think she likes me...*

Hopping in his truck, he sang a little tune until he got home. Caesar checked everything out, and Tim made sure to lock the gates. Closing up the chickens, they went inside for the night.

All looked good, and nobody had been there, except he noticed a note on his desk blotter. *"Things are not what they seem, beware."*

Darn, what did this mean? Looking around, Tim said out loud, "are you, Sean Gilroy?"

Tim felt the cold air, and that smell in the room, and on the pad came *"YES."*

Tim almost fainted as he sat down quickly. *I have a ghost! He wanted to ask more, but his office was bugged, so he let the questions pass at this time. But now he knew that the body was Sean Gilroy.*

Tim and Caesar quietly left the office, taking a notepad and shutting the door. *Darn, I don't know what to do or which way to turn.*

In the kitchen, he said out loud, "Sean, would you tell me what happened to you and a little about the amalgam and the map?"

No cold air, Caesar's ears didn't perk up, nothing happened.

"I can't talk to you in the office, as someone is listening. It's safe here in the kitchen."

Nothing. *Maybe Sean doesn't want to talk about it.* "Well, Caesar, let's go to bed, tomorrow is another day, and it should be fun. Let's see who comes to visit."

The lone person sat in the car down the road listening. Hearing Tim ask a person a question if he is Sean Gilroy? Interesting. But there was no one in the house, Tim is acting weird. He watches the lights go out in the house, knowing Tim is going to bed. It sounds like tomorrow we will find out more about what is going on.

Chapter Fourteen

Tim was up early to make his plan work. Grabbing a cup of coffee, he went into the office and sat down. Picking up the phone, he pretended to talk to someone, "Hi. I'll pick you up in an hour, and we'll see what we find." Pause. "Sounds good, see ya."

Grabbing an empty lunch bucket, the two of them headed for his pickup. As Tim was pulling out of the driveway. He noticed a tan car parked down the road a bit. *I wonder who that is? As I've never seen that car around here before.*

When he started driving from home to Highway 50, the parked car took off too. *Hmm, is that vehicle going to follow me?* Tim turns left onto Highway 50, watching the car behind him. But the car got caught in traffic. Tim slowed down, and sure enough, the car turn left too. *This is interesting.*

When Tim arrived at the Virginia City turnoff, he made a left and headed up to Virginia

City, so did the tan car about ten cars behind him. Seeing there was quite a bit of traffic, Tim passed a couple of cars on the flat, and right before climbing the hill, he quickly turned on a road that took him back to the Moon Light ranch, a brothel. Only locals know the way.

Pulling into a business parking lot, he waited. Ten minutes went by; no car, *so he had lost it, or the car wasn't following him. Tim, you have to calm down,*

Now taking the back road, he headed home. Parking his truck at his neighbors, Tim and Caesar walked home to wait.

The driver in the car behind Tim pounded on the steering wheel, *Darn, I lost him, where did he go? Well, I know he is not home, so guess I'll pay another visit. He is bound to leave some information about the map at home.*

Chapter Fifteen

Tim and Caesar hid in the pantry, with the door cracked. Tim didn't know how long they would have to wait or even if anyone would come.

Tim gave Caesar a rawhide bone to chew on to keep him from getting bored. Tim was reading a book about airmail arrows by an author he had read before. He thought *I am going to have to check these arrows out.*

Around nine, he heard the alarm vibrate on his phone. Caesar's ear perked up, and he started to get up, "Stay boy." Tim whispered.

The front door has a keyless lock, and it couldn't be picked. Tim wondered how they would get in? He heard the garage door go up... *what the heck*. The kitchen door to the garage wasn't locked. Caesar started to growl, but Tim gave him the silent finger to his lips. Caesar stayed quiet but on alert.

Tim could only hear one person, and he tried to see where they might be through the crack in the pantry door.

Bang, as something fell in the front room. *Well, at least it didn't break.* Thought Tim, then a light went off in his brain, *Dummy, you can watch the security video on your phone.*

It was a man all dressed in black, wearing a hoodie. Tim couldn't see the face. Caesar was shivering with excitement. He wants to go, Tim held him tight.

Who is this guy? He doesn't resemble anyone I know.

The man went into the bedroom and started opening drawers, dumping things out and mumbling to himself. Leaving the bedroom, he goes to the office, sits at the desk, and turns on the computer. "Damn its password-protected," as he slams the computer lid. Looking through the desk drawers and finding nothing. "Damn, he must have taken the map with him..." He stomped out of the office, but the camera got a good look at his face. Tim thought, *Got you.*

As the man came back to the kitchen, Tim let Caesar go and open the pantry door with his gun pointed at the individual. "Can I help you?"

"Shit." About then, Caesar grabbed the man's hand and knocked him down.

"If I were you, I stay there while we wait for the police." Caesar didn't let go. Tim called 911 and told the dispatcher he had caught a burglar.

The Sheriff's unit arrived twenty minutes later.

"I have everything on tape and a good clear photo of this guy." Turning to the guy, who was now handcuffed, Tim asked, "Who are you."

The man practically spat out the words with a slur, "your worst enemy." The man staggered like he was coming down from some kind of drug.

"How can you be my enemy, when I don't know you," laughed Tim.

The man struggled with the cops and said, "You'll see."

One of the Deputy's placed him in the back of their patrol car. While Deputy Brown, from the first break-in, took a report of the incident from Tim. The man had no identification, so he was referred to as John Doe. Brown took the videotape as evidence. Tim thought *that was the best five hundred I ever spent.*

"I can't figure out how he got into the house through the garage? I had the front door lock change from the last break-in. I thought I had everything covered," said Tim.

Deputy Brown responded, "We found a garage decoder on him, so I suspect he has done this before."

"That's interesting. What happens next?" Tim asked.

"He'll be booked and fingerprinted, which we will run through NCIC to identify him. Then he is assigned an attorney and goes to court. Pretty cut and dry," replied the Deputy.

"Not for me it isn't, I want to know who he is," replied Tim.

"Call our office in a couple of days, and they should be able to tell you that information," stated Brown, handing Tim a copy of the report.

"Thanks, officer, for your prompt response to this," sighed Tim. "As you know, this is my second break-in in a month. The worst part there is nothing to steal."

"It's a good thing you invested in the security system this time. Well, let's hope this is the end of it."

'Me too."

Brown got in the vehicle, and they drove off. *Well, this was an exciting day. I love it when a plan comes together.*

Chapter Sixteen

The lone figure sitting in the tan car parked behind some large sage watched the goings-on. *Who was the man in the hoodie sneaking into Tim's house?* The man made a lot of noise in the house looking for something.

When the man went into the office, the listener heard louder noises and could tell he was going through the drawers, then the man said, "he must have the map with him"... *Interesting about the map. How would this man know about it?* Thought the listener.

A short while later, the Sheriff's cruiser came and took the man away. *Shit. This was a trap. I have underestimated Mr. Tim.*

Tim went back into the house and started picking things up... *this is getting old. But I caught him. Now to get rid of the bug.*

Tim and Caesar walked into the office to straighten out the desk drawers when they felt the cold air and that awful smell. On his desk blotter, came, *"You got the wrong person."*

"What are you saying? He broke into my house to steal something," sputtered Tim.

"Things aren't what they seem."

Tim was concerned if Sean was right, he didn't want to say much, with the bug in the room. *Shit!! What do I do now?* Caesar and Tim walked out of the room and shut the door.

The listener thought to himself. *This guy is losing it. He's talking to someone, and there isn't anyone there, but his dog.*

Sunday came and went with no burglars. All was calm, too calm. Tim never heard a peep out of his ghost.

Tim thought *I'll call the Sheriff's office tomorrow to find out if they identified the guy.*

Chapter Seventeen

First thing Monday morning, Tim called the Sheriff's office and gave them the case number. "Were you able to identify the John Doe?" Asked Tim.

Tim heard the gal going through papers. "Are you Tim Ryan?"

"Yes, mam."

"Let's see, his name in Gregory Barnes lives in Fallon. Has several wants, so we will have him for a while."

"Thank you so much for the info. I don't know who he is or what Mr. Barnes wanted." As Tim hung up, he thought. *Wow, Barnes, the same name as the Doctor in Fallon and Sherri's brother-in-law. But why did he break into my house? Tim tried to think back. Did he tell the Dr. what he found? No, I know I didn't. We only talked about the jar. He had never told Sherri.*

Tim packed a light lunch as they were going out to eat. A rawhide snack for Caesar and some water. Today he decided he wanted to know more about Sherri, like her last name and where she lived if it caused an end to the relationship, better now than later. I know Fallon is a small town, but this is too much of a coincidence.

Tim and Caesar arrived right at ten, Sherri wasn't there yet. They decided to sit in the truck and waited for her as it was cloudy and cold out today.

Sherri arrived fifteen minutes later. "Sorry to be late, but we had a little family crisis," she said out of breath.

Tim couldn't help himself, "Sorta like your nephew getting arrested?"

A shocked look came across her face, "Well, yes. How did you know?"

"I'm the one who had him arrested for breaking into my house."

Sherri almost fainted, "I didn't know it was your house. I'm so sorry."

"What do you have to be sorry about?" inquired Tim.

"He's family, and you're a friend. This is embarrassing. He's been in trouble a lot. I think it has to do with drugs." She shook her head, "But I don't understand why he would try to steal from you?"

"I don't understand either. I've nothing of value. I gave all my late wife's jewelry to the kids. I believe he tried to break in a few weeks ago and then succeeded last week and again last night. The silly part was he didn't take anything. However, he has been looking for something."

Sherri lowered the truck tailgate and sat down. Her face was white. "I'm so sorry. I'm so sorry. He's old enough to know better. Damn, he's twenty-three."

"Why don't you tell me the whole story?" asked Tim.

'What do you mean?"

"How did he know where I lived for one? Your last name for two and where you live for three," suggested Tim.

"I don't know how he found out where you live, as I don't even know. I agree I haven't been upfront with you. I didn't know you, so I am cautious about letting people know who I am and where I live."

Sherri paused for a second, "Not sure how you are going to handle this. My last name is Gilroy, and I live at 2217 Platte Way. Does that help?" she said with a little sneer.

"Wow, Gilroy, this is a small world. Any relationship to Sean Gilroy?" snapped Tim.

"You are not going to like this. But, yes. He was my late husband Johnathan Sean Gilroy, great grandfather," stated Sherri.

Tim pushes his hair back, "This is unreal. The body I found in the outhouse hole that we suspected was Sean Gilroy after our trip to Hot Creek. Now I am finding out he was your husband's great grandfather... This is too weird."

"Yes, agreed. The only thing I can think of is I had dinner at my brother's house right after meeting you, and we talked about you finding a skeleton head and a jar that you tried to hide. Greg was there. Then after our trip to Hot Creek, it came out that you thought the body might be Sean. The family always wondered what happened to him. I'm so sorry for all of this," cried Sherri.

"You could have been truthful about Sean."

"Yes. I should have, but I didn't want to spoil our relationship," as Sherri put her face in her hands.

Tim didn't know what to say. He was hurt. "I believe I am calling it a day." Walking over to his truck with Caesar, they drove off.

Sherri sat on her tailgate and cried.

Tim was more confused than ever. He was angry and hurt. He cared for Sherri more than he realized. But his mind was churning. Greg broke into his house, but Sean said he wasn't the right person. *Who else is after the gold or the map? I'm going to have a beer, hell I might have three. This day sucks!!*

Chapter Eighteen

Tim was still fuming when he hit the house. I knew the relationship was too good to be true. Damn, he really liked Sherri.

He went into his office and grabbed the listening device, "Listen here, you, whoever you are, leave me alone," and smashed the bug.

"Now, Sean, you and I are going to talk."

The air got cold, and it came with that smell. "I know you are in here." Walking to the kitchen, Tim placed the pad on the table. "Here is a writing pad. Tell me your story," demanded Tim.

Nothing.

"I deserve to know the truth, finding that jar has brought me nothing but sadness."

"*I tried to warn you. Told you things aren't what they seem.*" Came the writing.

"Awe, come on, give me the truth, not a bunch of crap."

Nothing.

Tim hit the table and walked out of the room, Caesar followed.

Writing started to appear on the pad. "*It all started when I was a little boy. My mother told me to grow-up, or I would never amount to anything, and be just like my father.*"

The listener, though, *damn, he found the bug. How do I get in and plant another? I have to find that map, or there will be hell to pay.*

Tim walked back into the kitchen and saw what Sean had written on the pad. *Great, now I have a ghost with a dry sense of humor.*

"Okay, Sean, I know you are here, enough of this, let's get to the truth."

"But it's boring... "

"That's okay. I could handle some boring info, right now."

"Alright. I arrived in Lahontan City late in 1911. I loved the little town, plus I met this gorgeous woman and fell madly in lust... I mean love. We got married and had a son. But after a couple of years, my eyes wandered, and I seduced a married woman. Seeing there was going to be trouble. I took the amalgam and map of the mine and was running off. I got as far as the outhouse, throwing the jar in there for safekeeping, Figurined I would come back to retrieve it. Well, that didn't

happen, and you know the rest of the story."

"Do you know who killed you?" asked Tim.

"I believe it was the married lady's husband."

"Darn Sean talking to you is like pulling teeth. Who was her husband?"

"I believe his name was... I also think it's his relatives that are trying to get my gold and map now."

Ring, Ring, the darn phone was ringing in his office. Tim ran in and grabbed it. "Hi."

"Hi, Dad, it's Jeff. Just checking on you. I heard your house got broken into the other night. Is everything okay?"

"Hi Jeff, all is okay. How did you hear about it?"

"Well, it wasn't from you," as he laughed. " I read it in the Sheriff's blotter.

"Yeah, they got the guy, some punk from Fallon. I've nothing to steal, but my TV and computer. Everything of value I gave to you kids," sighed Tim.

"How have you been? We were hoping to come to visit. How about Wednesday night, around six? We will bring dinner," question Jeff.

"Sounds good. I would love to see you guys. The kids are growing so fast. Mary's, what twelve now? And Riley's eleven. Come around six. I have fresh eggs for you guys."

"Love you, Dad, see you Wednesday."

"Love you guys." Tim puts the phone down. He blamed himself for not seeing his kids that much. *I have become such an introvert.*

Jeff lives in Reno. Mark in Jackson, California, and his daughter Jessica in Susanville, California. All within a couple of hours drive. *I have to make an effort to see them from now on at least once a month.*

By the time Tim went back to the kitchen, Sean was gone. *Darn, who is the murderer? And why in today's world, do they want the gold?* Tim hit himself on the head. *Hey, stupid, what do you think, gold at eighteen hundred dollars an ounce, also they want the map.*

Chapter Nineteen

By Tuesday morning, Tim felt terrible that he had been so hard on Sherri. But darn she hadn't been foreright with him. *Well, Tim, you weren't honest with her either. That's different. Isn't it?* As his brain argued.

He decided to look up her phone number now that he knew her last name. It was easy to find, Sherri Gilroy 775-556-4695. *Shall I call her... I am not sure what to say. I have to think about it.*

"Come on, Caesar, let's eat breakfast."

Caesar came running as Tim fried them eggs. As Tim sat eating, he starts thinking about everything that is going on and writes it down on the pad left from last night.

1. Fell in a hole and found amalgam
2. Discovered the head
3. Met Sherri Gilroy
4. Met Dr. Barnes
5. The first time, did someone come to the house to get in? And who?

6. Had amalgam assayed
7. Found it came from around Hot Creek
8. House broke into and a bug planted
9. Visited Hot Creek and learned of Sean Gilroy
10. Found that the ghost is Sean
11. House was broken into again by Dr.Barnes's son
12. Sherri is related to everyone.

Shit, this doesn't tell me anything that I don't already know... where am I going with this? Tim puts his face in his hands and pushes back his hair... *I'm so frustrated. I wish I never fell in that damn hole. I still have more questions than answers.*

I think it is time I meet with Sherri and get all the truth about everything on the table. It will mean I have to tell her the truth too... am I ready for that? Darn, I already care for her more than I wanted.

Tim walked into his office and called Sherri.

The phone rang once, twice, "Hello." Came Sherri's voice.

"Hi, Sherri, this is Tim."

"I know, I have caller ID," she said softly.

"Thank you for answering. I wanted to apologize for yesterday. I'm sorry, but I was hurt and angry."

"Apology accepted, and please accept mine. I should have told you the truth."

"Could we meet and resolved this whole incident?" asked Tim.

"I would like that, plus I owe you a dinner," they both laughed.

They agreed to meet at Jerry's Restaurant in Fallon at six that evening.

Chapter Twenty

Tim decided after watching the locksmith, he could put in the new lock in the kitchen door. He had enough time to run into Home Depot and get the keyless lock. He usually never locks that door, but after all the going on, he just wanted to be sure no one else gets in the house.

He also made sure the writing pad and map were in the safe. Tim wasn't ready yet, for anyone to find out about Sean.

Around five, Tim and Caesar headed out for Fallon.

The tan car watched as Tim left. *Now to make a quick visit.*

The individual walked down to Tim's house, climbed the gate. Wearing a bandana over their face and sunglasses so as not to be identified.

Once inside the yard, trying the front door, keyless lock, I can't pick that. Going to the garage, the listener took out a decoder to open it. *Easy peasy. Damn, the kitchen door has a keyless lock too. Now how do I get in?*

Walking around the house, checking all the windows. Locked. *Should I break a window? Darn, I don't want him to know I broke in. Mr. Tim, you have gotten smart.*

Looking around, the listener spots a small covered window air conditioner, and it looked like it's on the wall of Tim's office. Uncovering the cooler, the listener pulls off the back cover with some effort, *glad I have a knife.* The listener places the bug inside. *This isn't great, but this time of year, it won't be running water through it, and I should be able to hear some things. I want to get back inside... next time.*

Tim arrived at Jerry's with five minutes to spare. Even with all the road construction, he made good time. Right at six, Sherri pulled up beside his truck.

"Glad you made it safe, with all that darn construction going on," stammered Sherri.

"Not a problem. Glad to see you. I wasn't sure if you would come," whispered Tim.

Sherri came over and hugged him, "Let's talk this all the out."

Sounds good to me." As they walked into the restaurant.

Chapter Twenty-One

They two of them sat down at a table in the back, with no one around.

Tim says, "I'll start. When you found me in the hole, I spotted a pickle jar, in fact, the one that cut me. It had amalgam and a map in it. I didn't want you to know about it mainly because I didn't know you."

"I understand. Amalgam is worth a lot of money," sighs Sherri.

'Yes, about fifty-five thousand. Anyway, I found out it came from somewhere around Hot Creek. That was why we took the trip. I got lucky when Gene told me the story or myth about Sean."

About then, the waiter came over and took their order.

"Remember this is my treat," Sherri said. And they both laughed.

"Now, this is where it gets weird. The head found in the outhouse hole, as you know, probably is Sean. Well, he is at my house, and he told me he is Sean."

"What??" said Sherri in disbelief.

"Plus, my house has been broken into two times, and I had an intruder once. The last break-in was your nephew. During the first break-in, they didn't take anything, just bugged my house. The house was in disarray, but I believe now that was a ruse." Tim took a breath, "And you won't believe this, it was Sean who told me about the bug."

Sherri looked at him, shaking her head, "This sounds like a sci-fi movie."

"I know. Apparently, this ghost has a dry sense of humor... Damn, I sound weird."

Sherri grabbed his hand, "Know it sounds like you have been through a lot. Now I understand why you got upset with me. I should have been truthful, and we could have worked this out together in the beginning."

Tim felt like a weight had been lifted off his shoulders, "Well, let's work together now to solve what is going on."

"Sounds good, replied Sherri.

Their food arrived, and they dug in. It was so good. They didn't talk for a few minutes as they digested their food and the conversation they just had.

"Now it's my turn to tell you about my family," commented Sherri. "As you know, my late husband's Great Grandfather was Sean Gilroy. We had heard the stories about him being a womanizer and that he had a map to a mine somewhere."

Sherri stopped for a moment as the waiter came by to see if they needed anything.

"I believe that's why Greg broke into your house to find the map. Which it sounds like he didn't, thank goodness."

"No, the map and the amalgam are safe," commented Tim. "Technically, I believe the amalgam is yours, seeing you were related to Sean by marriage."

"Maybe, but after so many years, it is finders keepers." They both laughed.

"Interesting point. Sean was going to tell me the other night who murdered him but didn't. He thinks it's their relative that is trying to find the map besides Greg."

"How did you end up with Sean?" Asked Sherri.

"That is a good question. I don't know. Sean just showed up and is keeping an eye on me. I'm hoping when this is resolved. He will pass over," volunteer Tim.

The waiter came with the bill, "I'll be your cashier whenever you are ready." he stated.

Tim went for his wallet, and Sherri said, "This is my treat, remember. You can get the next one." *Tim likes the sound of that. There will be a next time.*

"We need to come up with a plan to catch whoever is behind the break-ins and resolve the murder of Sean," stated Tim.

"Let's go to my house and discuss this further, as we do need a plan." requested Sherri.

"Sounds good, but I think I will pass, for now, I want to get more info out of Sean," explained Tim.

A hurt look came across her face, "I understand."

"I didn't mean to hurt your feeling, but Sean is the key to all of this."

"I agree, I just wanted to spend more time with you," whispered Sherri.

The got up and walked out of the restaurant to their trucks. However, they're leaving didn't go unnoticed.

Tim gave her a big hug and kiss on the cheek, "I will call you tomorrow."

Sherri hugged him back, "I'll wait for your call."

Tim let Caesar out to go pee and gave him the treat he had in his pocket. They both got into the truck, waving goodbye to Sherri as he headed home.

Sherri stood by her truck for a minute thinking, then got in and drove away.

Chapter Twenty-Two

Driving into his driveway, all looked okay. He didn't see the tan car or any car parked down the road. Now to talk to Sean.

Turning on his computer, Tim said, "it's time to talk."

In the office, he felt the cold air and that smell. Writing appeared on the desk pad. *"Not safe in here, something is in that brown box in the wall. Not sure what it does or how it works."*

"What the heck? It's an air conditioner to help cool the room." Tim reached over and turned on the air conditioner to show Sean how it worked. It made a terrible sound. *Darn, it's still covered for the winter, and the water is turned off.* But he left it running.

Sean wrote again on the desk pad, *"one of those devices like in the ivy plant is in the brown box."*

Is this ever going to end... who is listening? Thought Tim. Taking a flashlight, he goes outside to see what is in the air conditioner. Sure enough, another bug.

The listener, saying out loud, "Damn, how did he know it was in the air conditioner? Well, if I can't listen in, I will have to confront him sooner or later. Damn, this shouldn't be this complicated."

Going back into his office, Tim sat and looked at his phone. There on the video was a person wearing glasses and a bandana covering their face. The build was slight. Tim couldn't tell if it was a man or a woman. They also opened his garage, *darn these decoders must be everywhere.*

Tim thought *this person is getting brave. I am going to have to be prepared.*

"Okay, Sean, it's safe to talk. I want the rest of the story. Who killed you?"

The cold air and smell came into his office. Caesar's ear perks up.

Writing started to appear on the desk pad. *"It's so dull, and it happened ninety-some years ago. I'll have to say that the woman was amazing in bed... But come to think about it, not that amazing to get killed over."*

"Enough with the crap and get to the point," snarled Tim.

"Okay, Okay, I was having a beer at the bar, when the husband came in looking for me, he didn't see me at first, so I quietly sneaked out the back door.

However, he saw me and came running. I wanted to grab my horse and get out of town. Seeing I wasn't going to get away, I quickly threw the jar in the outhouse. I figured he would beat me up, and I would gather it later. Well, he came at me with a baseball bat, and I guess he threw me in the outhouse to die, which I did. End of story."

"Not quite, who was he?"

"Some Irish gent by the name of O'Leary," replied Sean.

Tim rubbed his head. *He didn't know anyone named O'Leary. Plus, the family now may have a different name. So I'm still at square one.*

Chapter Twenty-Three

The next morning, he called Sherri and told her what he had learned. I need to find a person who understands genealogy.

Sherri became all excited, "I know someone. She used to come into the library all the time, researching old books and newspapers. I will call her and see if she can see us. Let me call you back."

A few minutes later, the phone rang, "She will see us at one, here in Fallon."

"We'll be there. Maybe we'll solve this matter... lets hope. Also, I am going to look on the computer,"

Time fired up his computer and put the name O'Leary in google, and a page called Library Ireland came up. *Shit, this is so confusing. Hopefully, this lady can help.*

At noon, Tim and Caesar headed for Fallon, with the tan car way behind them. Tim wasn't even paying attention. He was thinking about the branches of the O'Leary family.

The listener followed him to a green house, parking down the street. Within a few minutes, Tim and the former librarian came out all excited and hopped in Tim's truck. *Interesting that she is involved.*

Tim told Sherri that he tried the computer, and it was too confusing. Hopefully, this lady can help.

Sherri said, "Mrs. Placer is a little eccentric and loves cats. She has about twenty of them."

"Wow. So she is a cat lover. I'll make sure Caesar says in the truck," Tim laughs.

"Let me do the asking, if you don't mind, as she knows me."

"Not a problem, since you are a cat person." They both laugh.

Mrs. Placer lived in the older part of Fallon in a small bungalow. Her yard had lots of rose bushes, not yet in bloom. A lovely small porch with a rocker on it. The house was small but in great shape.

Sherri and Tim walked up to the front door and rang the bell.

The listener had followed them, parking down the street, and wondered why they were going to Mrs. Placers' house.

Mrs. Placer came to the door, a short, gray-haired woman in her seventies, all of five feet wearing a sunflower apron, wiping her hands.

"Come on in, I was making some sugar cookies for us," she said with a big smile. "I don't get company much, so this is a treat."

Walking into her cute little house with the aroma of cookies, it reminded Tim of his grandmother, except there were cats everywhere. Must have been twenty.

116

They follow her into her dining room. Her dining room table was covered with boxes of genealogy stuff, but one end had tea and the cookies. "Please have a seat. Now, what can I help you with?"

Sherri started, 'We are trying to break down the name O'Leary for the last eighty years or so, we need the different branches, as we suspect the person is no longer an O'Leary."

"Interesting. I knew of an O'Leary family that at one time lived at Lahotan City," replied Mrs. Placer.

'You knew the family?" asked Sherri, amazed.

"Heaven's no, I knew of the family, Edith, and Frank. I thought it would be interesting to do a background on them. I don't know why I picked them, maybe because I liked the name."

Mrs. Placer paused for a moment, "They had a son who married... let me think. Susan Mercer, that's it."

"Wow, what a memory you have," declared Sherri.

"Let me look. I believe they had two children, a son, and a daughter." She forges through some pages. "Yes, here it is. The daughter was named Mary, and the son was George. George was killed in the Korean War, or was it WWII? That I am not sure about. Mary married Stu Anderson and had two children, also a son and daughter." She stopped and took a sip of tea and nibbled on a cookie.

"Now let me see," as she rummaged through some more pages. Her son was Luke Anderson. He was killed in Afghanistan in 2003. The daughter, Nancy, married, dang can't find that information. Gotta be here somewhere." She rifles through more pages. "Oh, here we go, Nancy married George Stomper and had three children, two girls, and boy. Dang, I don't have their names. I will keep looking for you. Do you think we are on the right track? O'Leary was a pretty common name." Asked Mrs. Placer.

"Yes, it is, however, there couldn't have been that many in Lahontan City," replied Sherri. Sherri thought for a moment, "You know Stomper, that name sounds familiar. I know it from somewhere. Darn, I can't think of it, oh well it will come to me at three in the morning."

"That happens to me, too," she laughed. "I followed this family name because they had lived in Lahonton City. I thought they might be interesting," sighed Mrs. Placer.

"Glad you did. You have been a big help. We at least know their last name, Stomper. That is not a common name," chimed in Tim.

"I will keep looking," as she drank another cup of tea and nibbled on another cookie.

They all quietly sat around the table, eating cookies and drinking tea. Finally, Tim says, "Well, we best be going. I have Caesar in the car. May I take a cookie to him?"

"Please let me pack some up for you. Otherwise, I'll just eat them," she laughs.

They thanked her again for her help and her hospitality. She walked them to the porch and said, "Goodbye, I'll contact you, Sherri, if I find any more info."

They waved goodbye to her as they drove off. Caesar was munching on the cookies.

"It's a good thing Caesar didn't go in with all those cats." Tim laughed,   "You don't have that many do you?"

'Ha-ha, no, I only have two. Buster and Beatrice."

The listener followed.

Chapter Twenty-Three

"Well, we learned a lot today," as he was driving Sherri home. "Would you like to go for dinner? I know it is only around four."

"Sound great, but maybe a salad, something light, I am not too hungry," smiled Sherri.

"How about Pizza? We can get a small vegetarian," suggested Tim.

"You're on. Let's go."

Caesar likes the idea of food, no matter what kind or time of day. He sat there with a big smile. *Maybe they will give me another cookie.*

While waiting for the pizza, they talked about the information Mrs. Placer had given them. Tim googled Stomper and came up with boots, toys, but no name. He finally found a page called My Heritage. It was a great site, but Tim couldn't get any info for someone born between 1980 and 1990. The web page was more for their mother or father.

The pizza was delivered to the table, and it hit the spot, just the right amount. Tim wrapped a piece for Caesar.

Tim hated to go, but he had to close the chickens and chores at home. Dropping Sherri off, they planned on seeing each other Thursday as Jeff was coming over tomorrow with his grandkids. He gave her a big hug and a kiss this time. "Thank you for all the help,"

"Anytime, if that's my reward." They both laughed. One final hug and back in the truck, he went. "See you Thursday," as they waved goodbye.

On the drive home, Tim was on cloud nine, and Caesar was pretty happy too eating his pizza.

The listener wondered what the two of them were up to at the old lady's house. Well, there's only one way to find out. Let's go visit Mrs. Placer. *If I*

remember right, she loved genealogy. Maybe she will know who's Sean Gilroy's relatives.

When they got home, all looked okay. Tim checked his camera video, nothing. So that is good. Tim would ask Sean later about Edith and Frank to see if they were on the right track.

Closing up the chickens and making sure all the gates were shut, Tim went into the house. He fed Caesar and grabbed a beer. Tomorrow he would go to town and buy treats for the kids. He was excited about them coming to visit.

Going into his office, he called on Sean. Nothing. He sat at his desk and had a few swigs of his beer and said, "Sean, come out, come out, where ever you are."

The cold air came into the room with that smell. Writing started to appear on the desk pad. "*I don't want to talk.*"

"Tell me about Edith?"

"Oh, a fine young lass she was and amazing in bed."

So her husband Frank is your killer?

"Something like that, I don't want to talk about it."

That's okay. I found out what I needed to know.

"Good, with that, I wish you adieu." The air warmed up, and the smell disappeared.

Wait until I tell Sherri.

Around eight that night, the phone rang. It was Sherri. "Hi,"

"I just got a call from my brother-in-law. They brought Mrs. Placer into Emergency. She is in a coma, as she was severely beaten."

"What? Who would do something like that to that sweet old lady?" Asked Tim.

"I guess the cats raised enough of a ruckus that the neighbors almost caught the person. He or she drove off in a tan car. The Sheriff's office is looking for them."

"You said a tan car. The other day I saw a tan vehicle parked down the road from my house, and it followed me until I lost them. Wonder why they would beat up Mrs. Placer?" thinking for a moment, "because we went to see her, I bet," summarized Tim.

"Well, we are not sure it was the same car."

"True, but I would bet on it," commented Tim. "Damn, who would beat up a sweet lady, and why?" repeating himself.

"Dr. said he would keep me informed on how she is doing. Maybe we can talk to her when she comes out of the coma. That would answer a lot of things," sighed Sherri.

"On another note, it was Frank O'Leary that killed Sean, " stated Tim. "So, we need to find those first names that go with Stomper to put a stop to this madness. Then again, they may not be behind it,"

The listener was upset, *Shouldn't have lost my temper on the old bat. Damn, I was almost caught. Stupid cats! Must have been twenty of them.* The cat scratches had stopped bleeding, but they stung like heck. *All this and Mrs. Placer wouldn't give up any information, crazy women. I've got to get rid of this car. Hopefully, she dies before she identifies me. I have to be more careful.*

Chapter Twenty-Four

Wednesday morning, Tim and Caesar went to town to buy goodies for his grandkids. He was excited to see them as he hadn't seen them since Christmas.

Tim stopped at Best Buys and purchased some new games for the Xbox. At Costco, he loaded up on cookies, fruit, and a big chocolate cake for dessert.

He arrived home before twelve and called Sherri, "how is Mrs. Placer doing?"

"They now have her in a medicated coma, but she is getting stronger. The Doctor says it may be a week or so before she can talk as her jaw is broken too."

"Again, I ask, who would do such a thing to a sweet old lady? Did they find the tan car?"

"Not yet. But if I were that person, I would ditch it," proposed Sherri.

"Yeah, that would be the wise thing to do. Let me know if you hear anything. As you know, my kids are coming tonight for dinner. It will be sort of a relief to have a change in venue. I haven't seen them in a few months. So I get to play Grandpa. By the way, I have never asked, do you have children?"

It was quiet on the other end, "I have a son and a daughter, they both live out of state," she said nothing more.

Tim dropped the subject, "Well, I will let you go, keep in touch."

They said their farewells. "Bye." As Tim put the phone down, he thought, *wonder why she doesn't want to talk about her children? She's a woman of mystery.*

The day went fast. However, Tim would have liked it to go more quickly, as he genuinely was excited about seeing his family. Caesar knew something was up, but just wasn't sure what was going to happen.

Around six, Caesar's ears perked up, and he ran to the door. They had company. The storm door was open so that he could see out the window. The tail started wagging enough to shake his whole pit bull body. Tim opened the door, and Caesar went running out to greet the family. Everyone gave hugs and tried talking all at once. Tim helped them carry the food inside.

"How has everyone been? You kids have grown a foot since Christmas. I can't believe it has been over five months since I've seen you guys," whispered Tim.

"I know, and we live so far away," replied Jeff.

"I just don't go that way, as it's the big city." Tim laughed.

"Well, with the new freeway, you can make the trip in under an hour," commented Alice, Jeff's wife.

They put the food on the table as Tim took down the plates. Mary got the silverware and glasses. Jeff had brought roasted chicken, *one of Tims's favorite*, coleslaw, and mashed potatoes.

"Plus, we have chocolate cake and ice cream for dessert."

The kids cheered as everyone dug in.

After dinner, the kids and Caesar went to play on the Xbox. Tom thought *do I tell Jeff what is going on, or will he think I'm nuts*

"A couple of weeks ago, I went bottle digging out at Lahontan City," started Tim. "I fell in an old outhouse hole."

"Dad, you have to be careful. Did you get hurt?" Asked Jeff.

"I had to have some stitches, as I fell on a broken jar. But the point of my story is a woman rescued me. Her name is Sherri, and I've been seeing her ever since."

"That's great, Dad, you've been alone for too long," chimed in Alice.

"Well. We'll see. All of this is a little out of my comfort zone, but I do like her. I think you guys will too. The only downfall," Tim laughs, "She likes cats." Everyone laughed.

"Well, there is more to tell. I found inside the jar that cut me amalgam and a map of a mine. I believe that is what they were after when they broke into my house."

"Dad, do you have the amalgam in a safe place, as that is worth some money?" stated Jeff.

"It is safe. But Sherri and I are trying to find out who else broke into the house beside the guy I caught."

"You mean your house has been broken into twice?" asked Jeff.

"Yes. The crook planted a bug in the office."

"Dad, this sounds like a nut job."

"Oh son, It gets crazier. It would be best if you didn't think I've lost it. But I have a ghost that came with the gold."

Jeff and Alice both looked at him and shook their heads. "Dad, there is no such thing as a ghost."

"That's what I always thought, but believe me, I have a ghost, and he is protecting me! He's the one who told me about the listening devices."

The look of disbelief was still on their faces. "I know this is a lot to digest, but it's true," sighed Tim. "Your old man is not losing it, trust me."

"Dad, I believe you think it is true."

About then, the kids came running back into the room. "Grandpa, your front room is cold and has a terrible smell."

"That is Sean. He won't hurt you."

"Dad, enough of this! You will scare the kids," snapped Jeff.

Tim jumped up and said, "I am sorry you don't believe me, Son, but you should know that I don't lie. I was hoping you would understand what has been going on here. Sorry, I said a thing," sneered Tim. Tim started clearing the kitchen table. Everyone was quiet.

Alice got up to help him put the dishes in the dishwasher and packed up the leftovers. "You guys take them home with you as Caesar, and I won't eat them," he snapped.

"I sorry I upset you, Dad, but this is quite a story to digest."

"Yeah, I guess it is," sighed Tim. "But it's the truth."

The kids packed up their goodies and gave Tim a big hug. "We miss you, Grandpa." Tim almost cried. "I miss you guys too. I promise I'll come and visit soon."

Everyone got up to go. Jeff hugged his dad, Alice kissed him on the cheek. The kids all gave him big hugs as they headed for the car.

Caesar and Tim stood in the driveway and waved goodbye. After they left, they went down and shut the main gate, closed up the chickens, and headed for the house. *Well, that didn't turn out as I planned...*

In the kitchen, Tim felt the cold air and the smell. "Hi, Sean."

The writing pad was on the buffet, so Tim put it on the kitchen table with a pen.

Writing started to appear. "*I am sorry for all the problems I am causing you. But you are my only hope to resolve this matter so that I may cross over.*"

Well, Sherri and I are working on it and getting close. We know the last name of O'leary's relative. So that is something."

"You are blessed with a wonderful son and grandchildren. I never appreciated what I had. I turned out like my Dad… a liar and a louse."

"If you weren't a ghost, I would share a beer with you," as Tim gives a heavy sigh.

"Good night, Tim."

"Goodnight, Sean."

Chapter Twenty-Five

Tim gave Sherri a call, "Hi Sherri. Good morning, I was checking up on how Mrs. Placer was doing?"

"Well, she's still hanging in there, but it doesn't look good. She took a severe beating to her body and being in her late seventies. The Doctor felt they would know more in the next twenty-four-hours. If she doesn't get better then, they will transport her to Renown in Reno. I'm so worried for her."

"We have to find out who did this to her. Does she have children?" asked Tim.

A pause, "I'm not sure, but I think she once mentioned a daughter who lived somewhere in California. I guess we should try and notify her about her Mother."

"Plus, maybe she would let us into the house to search through her Mom's genealogy papers on the O'Leary's."

"Good point. I think I know where to locate Mrs. Placer's daughter's info. When I worked at the library, she checked out some expensive books, which generally we never let out. But it's a small town, and it was Mrs. Placer, so we made an exception. She had to fill out a form with all her information. I believe it may list her daughter. Let me check, and I will call you back."

"Sounds good, I will be home."

The listener was parked down the road in a gray pickup, watching to see what Tim was doing. The telescope gave a good view of the house, and the large sage bushes somewhat covered the gray truck, as it blended in. *I have to be cautious. Damn, I just want the map. It must be worth millions.*

The listener had grown up hearing about the myth. It was rumored that their great Grandfather killed Gilroy is a state of rage for sleeping with his wife. Gilroy had led his great grandmother, Edith, on about the riches, how they could live like millionaires, back then.

Gilroy had told her about the map to this gold mine somewhere around Hot Creek. Grandfather Frank never did find the amalgam or the map on Gilroy when they disposed of his body.

Now, Tim apparently has them both.

Tim fixed sausage and eggs for breakfast, and Caesar sat with his mouth-watering. The kitchen smelled of fresh perked coffee and cooked sausage. Tim loved to cook breakfast. When Molly was ill, he would take it to her in bed. *Damn, I missed that woman.* Tim thought about Sherri, *will she win my heart like Molly? Guess only time will tell.*

The phone rang, "Hi Mark, Are you calling because of my conversation with Jeff?"

"Yes, Dad. Maybe you have been alone too long. How about coming to live with us?"

Tim about threw the phone, " I am fine, sane, and quite capable of taking care of myself. Thank you for the kind gesture, but no!"

"Dad, don't be angry, we are just worried about you. A ghost in your houses protecting you. Now, doesn't that sound crazy."

"No. Because it is true, and have you guys ever known me to lie?" sneered Tim.

"No, I know you don't lie, maybe exaggerate a bit," Jeff laughed. "But I can't believe this. This ghost isn't a fish story."

"I am going to hang up now, believe me, or don't that is your choice, but I told the truth. I am pleased that you boys are worried about my sanity. Shit, I supposed you guys have talked to Jessica too."

"Yes, in fact, I am surprised she hasn't called already," replied Mark. "We don't like the idea that someone broke into your house. You're not safe."

"As I said before, I am safe and sane. I am sorry you don't believe or trust your old man. Goodbye son," with that, Tim hung up the phone.

Thank goodness I have caller ID. I won't answer unless it's Sherri. I thought my kids would believe in me. Boy, I blew that. I shouldn't have told Jeff, oh well, can't undo what's been done.

Chapter Twenty-Six

It wasn't until the afternoon that Sherri called back. In the meantime, the boys called again as well as Jessica. Tim darn near didn't answer Sheri's call.

"Hi, well, what did you find out?"

"Tim, are you sitting down?"

"Yes, I am sitting at my desk."

"Mrs. Placer never regained consciousness, and she has passed," whisper Sherri holding back her tears.

"Damn! I was so hoping she would make it. I feel guilty about her beating. I think we were followed to her house," sighed Tim.

"Do you really think someone was following us?" asked Sherri.

"Yes. It was whoever was in that tan car. I'd bet my life on it. Have they found the car?"

"Not yet. The good news is I got a hold of Mrs. Placer's daughter, and she gave us permission to review Mrs. Placer's papers. She will be at the house this evening around six, as she lives in Placerville. Her name is Louise."

"Well, that is good news. Maybe we can help Louise out with the cats and all. Plus, I bet the house is a mess," stammered Tim as he was thinking. *We need to warn Louise that she could be in danger.*

'I'll meet Louise around six at the house."

"Don't go there until I get there, it may not be safe," explained Tim.

"Wow. Do you think they would come back?"

"You never know. Who would have thought they would beat up an old lady. Damn, I wish I knew who they were. See you at six, and I'll pick you up."

"See you then. I never thought of them coming back... sort of scary," whispered Sherri.

Tim picked up Sherri at her house, and they drove over to Mrs. Placer's home. Louise wasn't there yet, so they sat outside and waited. Tim checked the area out for a tan car, but all he saw a few houses down was a gray pickup pulling up and parking.

"I wonder what her daughter is like, she sounded frail on the phone," quipped Sherri.

"Well. We know in a few minutes, that looks like her pulling into the driveway."

They both got out of the truck, locking Caesar inside because of the cats.

Tim walked up to the frail woman in her forties, "Hi. I'm Tim, and this is Sherri. I believe you talked to Sherri on the phone about us reviewing some of your Mother's genealogy papers."

"Oh, Yes. Yes, I did. I am Louise, but you know that" she said, a bit frazzled. "I am not sure what the house looks like. One of the neighbors said they tried to straighten it out as much as they could. Several of the neighbors took the cats. Two needed to go to the vet. I guess they put up quite a fight to protect my Mother," she whispered, choking back the tears.

142

"We are so sorry for your loss. Your mother was the sweetest person. I just can't imagine who would do this in our little town," sighed Sherri.

"Thank you. Well, let's go in and see what we see," mumbled Louise.

The neighbors did an excellent job of cleaning the house. It was hard to tell that a person had been beaten to death in there. The dining room table looked the same, papers scattered, with the rest of the boxes sitting at one end.

Tim thought *whoever killed Mrs. Placer didn't get any information from her, or they would have taken the genealogy records.*

"Do you mind if we go through your Mother's records?" asked Sherri.

"Please do, if it helps to find my Mother's killer, I am all for it," replied Louise. "If you don't mind, I'll leave you. I want to check on the rest of the house."

"By all means. We are sorry to be interfering. You probably have a lot on your plate right now?" said Sherri.

"I do, I need to take clothes to the funeral home for her to be buried in," Louise started to cry.

Sherri hugged her, "I can't imagine losing my mother this way. We will help you any way we can."

"Thank you." as she walked into the bedroom, still crying.

"The poor woman, this is so hard on her," cried Sherri.

Chapter Twenty-Eight

They each took a box to search through. There were six boxes and two albums. Neither one talked as they read all the documents.

After about an hour, "Here's info on Frank and Edith, in this box," explained Sherri.

They both started going through it very carefully. "This also looks like all the info on the Stompers," sputtered Tim, "we must be getting close.

"Here is a birth certificate on a Lisa Stomper, born in 1981, so that should fit the timeline," proposed Sherri.

Tim digs more in-depth in the box, "well, well, here is a 6th-grade school report card for a Bruce Gilbert Stomper in 1993, so he would be the youngest. No, wait, were they twins?"

"That's an interesting question. Maybe we will find out. Darn, I wish Mrs. Placer hadn't died, as she probably would have known," mentioned Sherri."Anyway, we now have two names, Lisa and

Bruce. Lisa probably is married and has a different last name. I hope we find the other girl's name," stated Sherri. " However, the name Stomper sounds so familiar, but darn, it won't come to me. But, for now, we have some names to work with if they're the ones behind all of this."

There was a knock at the door, "Louise, are you expecting anyone?" asked Tim.

"No. But it might be one of the neighbors?"

Tim yells out, "who is it?"

"Mrs. Butler, from next door."

Everyone relaxed as Tim opened the door.

A woman in her seventies with blue gray-haired came in. "I am Patti Butler. I just wanted to see how Louise is doing?"

Louise came out of the bedroom with red eyes. "I am holding together. How are you, Patti?"

"I am so sorry for your loss. I wanted to let you know that I have nine of the cats. They are doing fine. Vet Brown has two of the cats. One doesn't look like it will make it. But we will keep her in our prayers. The other eight cats are over at Mrs. Green's house, and they are also doing okay."

"Thank you so much for straightening up the house. You don't know how much I appreciate it. I am in the bedroom, trying to get her clothes for the funeral," Louise started to cry again. Patti gave Louise a big hug and started walking into the bedroom with her. "I will help you."

"Louise, before you go, we found some of what we needed. Do you mind if we take this box? I will gladly return it when we are done," explained Sherri.

"What did you find?"

"We rather not say as we don't want to put you in any danger in case they come back," warned Tim.

Alarmed came across Louise's face, "you think they will come back?"

"I wish I knew, but we want you safe," replied Tim.

"Louise, why don't you stay with me until this all over?" Said Patti.

147

"Okay," Louise stammered. All of this was overwhelming to her.

Tim and Sherri hug her goodbye and left with the box. Caesar was happy to see them. Tim knew the dog had to pee. "Hang on, boy, until we get to Sherri's house."

The listener watches them leave the house with a box. *What is in the box? They were in there for a long time. I wonder what is going on? Is the map in the box? Or information about the map or the relatives?*

The listener followed them.

Chapter Twenty-Nine

Tim left Caesar in the fenced-in front yard while they took the box into the house. Tim wasn't sure how Caesar would get along with Sherri's cats.

Sherri was greeted by the two cats when she walked in. One saw Tim and ran off to hide. "That's Buster. He is afraid of strangers."

Tim laughs, "Well, I don't think I am strange." Placing the box on Sherri's dining room table, he asked, "Do you have a phone book?"

"A phone book, you got to be kidding, do they still make those," she laughed.

Tim laughed too, "Yeah, I guess we do google everything nowadays." He got his cell phone and googled Bruce Stomper of Fallon, Nevada. No listing. "He must have an unlisted number or doesn't live here."

"Well, let us see what else we find in this box," stated Sherri.

The listener parked down the street and watched the house. *I could sneak up on them, except for that pit bull. Damn, I wish I knew what was going on.*

Caesar barked to come in. Sherri said, "You could let Caesar in to see how he gets along with Buster and Beatrice. They are used to dogs, of course, not one this big."

"Caesar is also used to cats, I used to have one, it was Molly's, but he died a few years back of old age.' Tim walked out and called, "Caesar, come on, boy, come on in." Caesar came a running. Tim grabbed him and said, "now be on your best behavior." Caesar looked at him and smiled.

Caesar sniffed around. Beatrice came out and sat next to the buffet, just observing Caesar and licking herself. Then she turned around and left.

150

Caesar laid down by Tim's feet, and that was that. Buster never came to see what was going on. "He doesn't like strangers, so it's common for him to hide," explained Sherri.

"Well, it looks like all is okay in the cat-dog kingdom," laughed Tim. They both smiled.

The listener thought, *now that the dog is inside, maybe I can sneak up and see what is going on.* With that, the listener walked up to the house and quietly opened the gate. He could see them at the dining room table, going through the box. However, he couldn't hear as the window was closed since it was May. The listener started walking around, looking for an open window. Not watching his footing, tripped on a flower pot. Caesar barked. *Shit.* The listener ran out of the yard, hearing Tim yell, "stop."

Tim saw the person running down the street. He couldn't tell if it was a kid or not, but he didn't think so. He looked for the tan car, but all he saw was a gray pickup. *Come to think of it, it looked like the one he had seen earlier on Mrs. Placers street.*

Tim quickly walked down the street to get the license plate when the truck turned around in the middle of the road and drove off. Tim did get part of it, Nevada plate BLT.

Tim hadn't seen the person get into the truck, *so maybe I'm just jumpy. But I will keep my eye out for that pickup in the future.*

Tim walked around the house to see if all was okay before walking back into the house. "I've never had anyone try to break into my house," stammered Sherri.

"It might have just been a kid, being nosy, and we are jumpy," said Tim trying to make light of the incident, as he smiled, but he was concerned.

They spent several more hours going through the box, finding nothing else.

Tim spoke up and said, "Well, it is after nine. I need to head home and feed Caesar, plus closed the chickens."

Sherri gave him a coy look, "You could spend the night here?"

Tim wasn't sure what to say, "I would love too, but not at this time. It doesn't mean I don't want to. I want the moment to be right and not us solving a murder."

"You're right. After we catch the bad guy, then we can concentrate on us," sighed Sherri.

"I like the sound of that." Tim gave her a big hug and kiss. "Now lock the doors after I leave and make sure all your windows are locked. I see you have a security system."

"Yes. Living alone, I got it years ago, never had much need for one. But after tonight, who knows?"

"Well, set it tonight."

Tim hugged and kissed her once more as he and Caesar went out the front door. He heard her lock the door. Tim thought, I *don't want anything to happen to her* as they got in the truck and headed home.

The listener thought *I was so careless. I was almost caught. Well, I'm going home to sleep on this problem and talk it over with family in the morning.*

Chapter Thirty

Tim was sitting drinking his coffee and reading the news on his tablet when his cell phone rang. It was Sherri. "Hi."

She was all excited. I found the last name, and it's Amy."

"How you find that info?" questioned Tim.

"I found it stuck to a piece of paper in an envelope. So now we have all three names, Lisa, Bruce, and Amy Stomper.   Darn, I wish it would come to me why I know that name."

"Do you mind coming over tonight so we can make a plan and have dinner say around six? I'll barbeque steaks. I want you to get to know the whole me," as he laughs.

"Would love it, I'll bring the rolls and salad."

"Gotta deal, see ya then." As he turned off his cell.

Tim got up and poured himself another cup of coffee when he noticed Mark's car pulls up to the gate. *I love my kids, but I'm not in the mood for this.*

"Sean, come out where ever you are, I'll need your help with this matter. You owe me." Nothing from the ghost. *Great.*

Tim didn't get up to let all three of the kids in, "the door is open."

"Hi, Dad," said Mark, "we aren't here to gang up on you." As they came in and grabbed a cup of coffee before sitting down at the kitchen table.

"Sure looks that way."

"Hi. Dad," the other two chimcd in. Mark, the oldest, of course, would do all the talking.

"Dad, we are all concerned about you. Your safety and your sanity. We want you to consider coming to live with one of us."

"I am fine. Thank you for your concern," snapped Tim.

"What about this ghost thing? You know there isn't any ghost," sighed Jessica. "Have you been drinking lately?"

"Yes, my clinical daughter, I have a beer now and then," sneered Tim. "However, I'm not one of your patients."

"Please consider the offer," whisper Mark.

About then, a terrible smell came into the room with cold air.

"Darn, guys, who farted?" asked Jessica.

Tim quickly puts the pen and writing pad on the table. "It's Sean."

Everyone looked at Tim in disbelief as the writing started to appear. *"Hello, my name is Sean Gilroy. I was killed in Lahontan City some ninety-years ago. Your Dad is helping to find my murder. They want my gold and the map to the mine."*

Everyone still sat there with their mouth open for a minute or two.

"Okay, Dad, that's a good trick, not sure how you did it, but I applaud you," laughed Jeff, the skeptic.

"I am way over here and nowhere near that writing pad, your sister is the closest," growled Tim.

"This is no trick. I am a ghost... face it! I may have been a lot of things in my living life, But now I am a ghost who wants to pass over. Believe your father!" as the pen was slapped onto the table.

Again, everyone sat there with their mouth open. No one knew what to say.

"I still don't believe it," said Jeff.

"How much proof do you need?" Asked Tim.

"I don't know, but there's no such thing as a ghost," snorted Jeff.

"Tim, your kids are blooming idiots. I stand in front of them, writing, and they don't believe it. What kind of kids did you raise?"

Everyone stammered, wanted to say something, but not sure what.

"All I can say is wow, Dad, you have a ghost," said Mark. Everyone shook their head in agreement. Jeff a little slower, as he was still skeptical.

"Thank you, Sean, for telling my kids how it is," sighed Tim.

"Thank you, and I will wish you all adieu." With that, the smell left, and warm air filled the room.

Everyone started talking at once, not believe what they just saw. "Dad, I am sorry for not believing in you. I know you never lie, but this was hard to imagine. Who would have ever thought a ghost was living with my father?" smiled Mark.

"I kept telling you I wasn't crazy. It was hard for me to digest at first. However, Sherri and I have almost solved the mystery."

"Tells us more about Sherri?" asked Jessica.

"Hopefully, you guys will get to meet her soon. We have a lot of fun and enjoy the same things. She is also a widow," beamed Tim.

The kids all smiled and thought, *looks like Dad has found a new partner.*

Jeff said, "I'm happy for you. Also, I will be happy for Sean when he passes over."

"Well, it was great seeing you guys, but I know you have quite a trip going home. Hopefully, the next time we get together, you'll meet Sherri."

The kids put their coffee cups in the sink and started to head home. "Before you leave, I have eggs." Tim puts two dozen eggs in each bag. With hugs and lots of love, they left with a lot to talk about with their family.

Tim and Caesar walked down and shut the gate. When Tim came back into the house, he said, "thank you, Sean, now we are even."

The listener sat down the road, watching the house with the telescope. He saw the people leave with bags. *Wonder what that was all about. I think*

I am going to talk with Mr. Tim soon, like maybe this evening. But first, I have to get rid of that dog.

Chapter Thirty-One

Tim took two excellent rib eyes out of the freezer, poured the marinade sauce over them, and let them sit covered. *Tonight Sherri will find out what a great cook I am.*

Tim picked the house up, even vacuum and mopped the floors. Plump up the pillows on the couch. Everything looked good. He was excited about having Sherri over. She had never been to his home.

Tim and Caesar went out and closed up the chickens, and then he fed Caesar. The day seems to be moving so slow. *Are you excited to see Sherri? Yes, I am,* thought Tim.

Caesar asked to go out, which is normal after he eats. Tim got up and let him out, as it was only five-thirty and not dark yet.

The listener saw the dog running around. This is a perfect time to get rid of him. He reached into an ice chest and pulled out a piece of meat in a baggie. The beef was treated with a light dose of Acepromazine, hopefully, enough to put him to sleep.

Hopping out of the truck and walking up to Tim's fence, the dog sees the person and came running; as the meat is thrown, the dog takes a smell then gives a big pit bull smile as he gobbles it up. Within minutes he is out.

A car is coming down the road, *shit, where do I hide.* The listener crouches down as not to be seen.

The truck pulled up to Tim's gate. The listener recognized the woman and started sneaking up behind her as she opened the gate.

Tim sees the truck at the gate. *Damn, I forgot to leave it open.* Going out through the garage, he sees a man sneaking up behind Sherri. Tim tries to yell. But the man has already put his hand around her neck and has a gun pointed at her ribs.

"Stay where you are, Tim," the man says.

Tim thinks, where is Caesar? What do I do now? Play it cool, as he could kill Sherri.

The man wearing a mask walks Sherri toward Tim, "Let's go into the house, shall we?"

Tim thought *I had heard that voice before... but where?* They all walked into the kitchen, and the man still has a hold of Sherri's neck, with the gun pointed at her back. Fear was written all over Sherri's face, but she stayed calm.

"Let's go get the map," said the masked man.

"It's in the office," replied Tim and started walking that way.

"The hell it is, I tore that place apart," snarled the man.

Tim smiled at the man, "You just didn't look in the right place." Walking over the shelves, Tim moved it aside, and there was a wall safe.

"Damn, I could have saved us a lot of trouble if I knew it was there."

"Yeah, like the murder of Mrs. Placer?" Sneered Tim.

"Just give me the map," demanded the masked man.

Tim opened the safe and retrieved the map, holding on to it before giving it to the man. "Before we die, can you answer some questions?" asked Tim.

"Like what?"

"Why did you kill Mrs. Placer? She was a sweet old lady."

"Not that it matters, cause it doesn't. It was Amy, as she lost her temper. She has a habit of doing that. Hell, she suffocated my five-year-old twin sister, because she was crying," ranted the man. "I do as she says, or she would kill me on a bet," the man vented.

Tim placed the map on the desk as the familiar order, and cold air entered the room. "God, man, what did you do, shit your pants?" yelled the masked man.

Tim just smiled.

"Well, it was great talking to you all, as he shoved Sherri over by Tim and pointed the gun to shoot.

The lamp floated in the air behind the man, then it crashed hard on the masked man's head, down he went, but not before he got a shot off, creasing Tim's shoulder.

Tim didn't feel it at the time, due to his adrenaline flowing, he grabbed the electric wire from the broken lamp and tied the masked man's hands behind his back.

All the time, he told Sherri to call 911.   Tim ran into the kitchen and got some twine to tie up the man's legs. Tim then took off his mask.

"Wow, that's Bruce from your bother in-laws' office."

Sherri whispered, "and Amy Stomper works at the vet's office, I just remembered."

Caesar came staggering into the house all wobbly, stumbling up to Tim. Tim grabbed his dog and gave him a big hug. It was apparent that the masked man had drugged the dog. At least thank goodness, he hadn't killed him.

Sherri said, "Tim, you are bleeding. Do you have a first aid kit around here."

"In the bathroom," he whispered, as now he was feeling the pain.

While she was gone, Tim heard the sirens stop at the gate, as the Sheriff had to move Sherri's truck before they could get in. Tim thought, *my neighbors are going to love me.*

Deputy Brown was the first one in, "Well, Mr. Ryan, we meet again. What do we have this time?"

"Bruce Stomper is the main man that has kept breaking into my house, and his sister killed Mrs. Placer. They did all of this for this map to a gold mine somewhere down by Hot Creek. Here is his gun. It will have mine and his fingerprints on it."

"You've been shot, do you want us to call an ambulance?"

"No. Florence Nightingale will fix me up. If you don't mind, I know it is not protocol, but I'll like to come by tomorrow and give a full report." The other deputies escorted Bruce to the patrol car.

"Normally, we don't do that, but in this case, I'll make an exception. I suppose you have a video of this man?"

"Sure do, showing him holding a gun on Sherri. And the video recording where he says his sister beat up Mrs. Placer," replied Tim. *Again, thinking that's the best five hundred dollars I ever spent.*

The officers gathered up all the evidence, saying, "I'll see you tomorrow morning."

"Will do, first thing in the morning," replied Tim.

Tim followed the patrol cars out and drove in Sherri's truck, shutting the gates.

What a night, and it is only eight, still time for dinner.

"You hungry, Sherri, for a steak, and we'll drink a beer while they are cooking."

"Believe it or not, I am starving, and a beer sounds mighty good."

Chapter Thirty-Two

The next morning, Tim was up cooking breakfast for two. It was a glorious morning.

"Good morning, something smells good," said Sherri as she shuffled into the kitchen wearing one of his shirts and poured herself a cup of coffee. Watching her stand by the kitchen sink, drinking it, make Tim thinks of Molly. I didn't know if I'd be lucky enough to find two women to be my soul mate.

"Sean, are you around? We need to send you on, though I am going to miss you."

Nothing.

Tim puts the writing tablet on the table, "before you go, I have some questions."

The smell came first, then the cold air. Sherri had never smelled it before. "Wow, what stinks?

"It's Sean, remember he was in an outhouse for ninety-plus-years," smiled Tim.

All of a sudden, a fog appeared in the kitchen, and there stood Sean. A tall, handsome, well-built man in his thirties, dressed in fine clothes. He had wavy brown hair and steel-gray eyes.

"Well, aren't you, dapper," laughed Tim.

Sherri was shocked, "Tim, he looks like my dead husband and son. The gene carried on through all these generations."

The writing started to appear. *"First, thank you both for finding the murderers."*

"Sean, thank you for saving our lives. But I wanted to know about the map... seriously, it looks phony."

"Ha-ha. It is. I created it. There's no gold mine. But the ladies loved the thought of being rich. Told you I was a liar and a louse."

"Then, where did the amalgam come from?"

"From an old miner who was dying. He was coming from the

Tonopah area when I found him out in the desert. He gave me the amalgam and his mule if I would bury him, which I did. That's when I thought I would draw up this map and make up a story to win the ladies."

Tim was looking at Sherri, "so the amalgam, seeing it's yours, should go to your family. Sean, meet your relative. This is Sherri Gilroy. She was married to your Great Grandson, Johnathan Sean Gilroy."

"Glad to meet you, most beautiful lady. It seems my family was lucky and had good taste in women. I am glad you are with Tim. He is a great person. I have put him through a lot."

Both of them blush. "Sean, I never thought I'd say this, but you were a great house guest. But now it is time for you to go over. You will be missed."

"And you to my friend. Until we meet again."

The fog and the image started fading away, along with the smell and cold air. "Goodbye, my friend," whispered Tim.

"Wow, no one will ever believe this," claimed Sherri.

"So true. Well, now we know the whole story, and the amalgam is yours. You are a rich woman. I figure it's worth over fifty thousand, and I have a buyer for it," explained Tim.

"Now, I'll wonder if you like me or if you are after my money," smiled Sherri. They both laughed.

"Well, we have to go make a police report for the Sheriff. Let's get dressed." As he pats her on the behind.

Chapter Thirty-Three

Summer blew by, and now it was Fall, Tim knew he was madly in love with Sherri. She had met his kids, and they loved her. But he had never met her children.

Sherri had come over for the day and was sitting at the kitchen table. Very quietly, she said, "I have asked my children to come and visit and meet you."

"Wow, you have never talked about them," stammered Tim.

"I know. Let me tell you why. Their Dad died when Sean was seventeen, and Susan was fifteen. That was over fifteen years ago. But they blamed me for his death when he died in a car accident."

Sherri had a sad look on her face and started telling her story again," We had a terrible fight about him being a womanizer and drinking too much. He took off in the car and crashed it on Mount Rose." She paused for a moment. "The kids felt it is was my fault and decided they wanted to live with my parents, instead of me. Over the first year, they hardly talked to me. But after a while, we finally reconnected. Basically, they have grown up, and I believe they figured out the truth about their Dad. It came to light that he had an illegitimate daughter by another woman."

Sherri took a breath, "Sean. My son is a computer guy and works in Simi-Valley, California. Susan went on to be a nurse and lives in Colorado. I supported them through school and college. Plus, I still help them out now and then."

"I am glad they are coming for a visit. Do the kids know about the money?" Asked Tim.

"I know what you are thinking, but money was never a problem. The one thing my husband did right was to leave us well off. No, I think they are coming home as they want to meet you," and she smiled. "They will be flying into Reno this afternoon. Do you mind taking your truck to pick them up as you have a back seat?"

"Not a problem. We'll leave Caesar home, as I have treats to give to him." Sherri gave Tim a big hug. "Thank you."

"Any time lady," as he bowed. Tim felt honored that they wanted to meet him.

Sherri was right. Sean looked just like the ghost Sean. He even had the same dry sense of humor. Susan was a lot like her mother, quiet and didn't talk a lot.

They spent three days with the kids. It had been years since they had seen beautiful Lake Tahoe and Virginia City. They went to dinner at the JT in Gardnerville for Basque food. Tim was proud to show them Nevada by taking them to all the tourist spots.

The three days flew by, and it was time for them to go home. Tim packed all their stuff in his truck bed. Sean was helping him. "Tim, it's a pleasure meeting you, and hopefully we will see more of both of you. I haven't seen Mom this happy in a long time."

"Well, thank you. I do care for your Mom a lot. Maybe soon we'll be married, and I would love it if you were my best man," said Tim. "But don't tell your Mom, as I haven't proposed to her yet, waiting for the right time." They both laughed.

"I would be honored. Thank you for asking," replied Sean. They each gave a man hug as the women came to the car.

"All packed and ready to go, we should make it to the airport with plenty of time to spare," said Sean.

The trip from Fallon to the Reno Airport is about an hour and a half. The girls sat in the back with the men in front. The conversation never stopped. The kids said they would plan on coming home for Thanksgiving. Tim said, "by then, the murder trial should be over, and our lives should be back to normal."

"I sure hope so," chimed Sherri.

Finally, they arrived at the airport and helped the kids with their luggage and stuff. Hugs and kisses flowed as they saw them off.

"I like your children. They are great," said Tim.

"And they liked you," smiled Sherri.

"You want to go someplace to eat as we are in Reno. I know a great barbeque place called "Brothers.""

"Sounds great, I love barbeque food." She winked and smiled at Tim.

Chapter Thirty-Four

The murder trial started the second week in October. Tim and Susan went every day, in case they called them as witnesses. As it turned out with all the evidence, Tim had given the D.A. They were not called.

The jury deliberated for one day and came back with first-degree murder for Amy Stomper for the death of Mrs. Placer, a senior. Attempted murder for Bruce Stomper.

Amy received life with the possibility of parole, and Bruce received twenty-five years. Tim and Sherri were pleased with the court's decision.

"They won't be hurting anyone for a long time," said Tim.

"Let's get one more day of bottle digging before the weather turns too cold," stated Tim.

"Sounds good, let's go Saturday," spluttered Sherri as she was drinking her coke.

Saturday morning, Tim was to meet Sherri at Lahonton City. It was a nippy day, typical October weather.

Tim drove over to the abandoned outhouse, which was now covered with dirt. Sherri drove up a few minutes later.

"Remember this spot," asked Tim.

Sherri laughed, "How could I forget, you found gold and a ghost."

"Well, there is something else about this spot. I met you. Now I want you to remember it even more," as Tim got down on one knee, "Will you marry me?"

Sherri had a look of amazement, "You bet. Did you think you were going to get away from me?"

Jumping up, he grabbed Sherri and swung her around. "Love you to the moon and back."

"I love you too, Mr. Ryan."

They were married Thanksgiving day in a small church. It was a simple ceremony, with all their family and friends. Sean was Tim's best man, and Jessica was Sherri's matron of honor.

Tim thought *I wish Sean were here to see this. It's all because of him.*

A cold breeze with *a* fog filled the entrance hall of the church, but with no smell. Writing started to appear, in the guest book,

"*Best of luck to you two,*

I will always be close by if you need me.

Your friend, Sean Gilroy."

Made in the USA
Columbia, SC
08 August 2021

42898708R00109